Tennessee Tales

Tennessee Tales

By Hugh Walker

Aurora Publishers Incorporated
NASHVILLE AND LONDON

8990

COPYRIGHT © 1970 BY
AURORA PUBLISHERS INCORPORATED
NASHVILLE, TENNESSEE 37219
LIBRARY OF CONGRESS CATALOG CARD NUMBER: 76-114778
STANDARD BOOK NUMBER: 87695-013-6
MANUFACTURED IN THE UNITED STATES OF AMERICA

Contents

Foreword

For more than twelve years, my family and I spent many of our weekends exploring the hills and hollows of Middle Tennessee. Through our travels we gained a better understanding of Tennessee and its people, who were always helpful and kind.

Most of our travels were on back roads, and many of the roads are still there. Some of the old hotels we visited at Red Boiling Springs are still there too—and as timeless as the face of the land itself. But many of the places and faces have changed. The old locks are gone from the Cumberland River, and the beautiful old stone bridge that was over the Elk River has fallen into the stream.

Articles about our travels and the people we met appeared in the Sunday edition of *The Nashville Tennessean.* Sometimes we retraced our steps looking for new stories, and we always found that there was another story to be written.

I want to thank the *Tennessean* for permission to use the articles in this book and Stanley Horn for his help and advice. I also want to mention three of the books that were so helpful—Eastin Morris's *Gazeteer of Tennessee* (1834), J. B. Killebrew's *Resources of Tennessee,* and Judge S. C. Williams' *Early Travels in the Tennessee Country.*

—Hugh Walker

Montgomery Bell

BELL'S TUNNEL:
A Visit to the Narrows of the Harpeth

"Hard as nails" and "tough as pig iron" are timeworn expressions which were coined to describe men like Montgomery Bell. Some people admired Bell; others didn't. In the quarter century before the Civil War, he was recognized as the greatest ironmaster in the western iron belt of Tennessee, an area covering all or part of thirteen counties (5,400 square miles). A line drawn from Florence, Alabama, to Clarksville, Tennessee, would pass through the center of this great ore belt, according to Killebrew's *Resources of Tennessee.*

Into this rough, broken country, about the year 1800, came a young Pennsylvanian, Montgomery Bell. A few years earlier he was a successful hat manufacturer in Lexington, Kentucky, but he was interested in water power and saw possibilities for profits in the West Tennessee hills.

In 1804 Bell bought Cumberland Furnace from James Robertson for $16,000. Every dollar he made seemed to make another one, and in a few years he owned three hundred slaves, thousands of acres of land, and nearly a dozen iron furnaces and forging mills.

Bell had a reputation for being rough on his slaves and for nonpayment of debts. It wasn't that he couldn't pay; he just wouldn't. In other fields, too, the ironmaster was no shining light. Corlew, in his *History of Dickson County,* says, "according to tradition Bell numbered among his illegitimate children both whites and blacks." Bell never married.

In his older years Bell softened somewhat. He named Whorley

1

Furnace, south of Dickson, for a trusted slave. He freed many
of his slaves and gave $20,000 toward the founding of Mont-
gomery Bell Academy that others might have the education
he never had. These good deeds did much to raise Bell in the
estimation of his neighbors in the years before his death in 1855.

Corlew refers to the "Narrows of Harpeth" as "the most
remarkable of all Bell's undertakings." Even now one cannot
help being impressed with the imagination and energy of the
man who conceived and carried out this feat of engineering.

The Big Harpeth is a fast-rising, fast-falling little stream that
curves through the Highland Rim from Kingston Springs on
toward the Cumberland. Bell noted that at the Narrows the
river made a great horseshoe bend around a steep hill, returning
on the other side of the ridge to within a hundred yards of
its course and flowing at a level that is nineteen feet below
the origin. He decided to dig a tunnel connecting the "upper"
and "lower" Harpeth at this point, compressing the six-mile,
nineteen-foot fall into sixty yards. He employed E. W. Atkisson
of Cheatham County to superintend the work.

Inside   Bell's   Tunnel,   looking   toward   the   waterfall.

Atkisson found construction of the tunnel rough going, but he had plenty of slave labor and completed the project within a year, probably in 1818.

A stream swirls through the black, cave-like tunnel. The stream is only a few inches deep on the smooth rock bed, but here and there small waterfalls have worn deep holes. On the lower side of the Harpeth, the stream falls from the tunnel on the site where Bell had his Patterson forge. Water from the tunnel continues for some distance before joining the lower course of the river.

Not far from the tunnel is Newsom's Mill, built by Jimmy Newsom in 1862, the year the Federals occupied Nashville during the Civil War—but this did not prevent Jimmy from building his beautiful mill on the Harpeth. Near the mill stood the great stone house built by Jimmy Newsom in 1857. It was surrounded by a beautiful wall of cut stone. Time did not damage the house, and nothing less than bulldozers and dynamite could tear down the century-old stonework.

*Newsom's Mill,
still standing,
was built in 1862.*

The haunted house of seven husbands.

GHOSTS WALK IN HAZEL GREEN

The village of Hazel Green, Alabama, is only four miles from the Tennessee line. A mile to the east of this village, on a good road, is the famous—or infamous—Jeffries house. Here lived Elizabeth Dale, the beautiful daughter of Adam Dale, first settler of DeKalb County, Tennessee, and founder of the town of Liberty.

Elizabeth Dale was eventually known as Mrs. Gibbons-Flannigan-Jeffries-High-Brown-Routt. The official *Alabama Guide Book* says she was "a fascinating lady of many marriages."

The huge old frame house stands on an Indian mound overlooking flat cotton fields, its back turned to one road and its side to another. It stands on the site of a log cabin built by Alexander Jeffries, an early settler.

Jeffries married the already twice-married Elizabeth Dale, whose first two husbands died mysteriously. (All that is known of Elizabeth is that she liked horses and expensive clothes.) Jeffries passed on very shortly; the cause of his death was unknown. Elizabeth soon married Mr. High, but again death made her a widow.

Elizabeth's fifth husband was Absolam Brown, who built the big house. He, too, soon died of unknown causes and was quickly buried by candlelight in the family cemetery.

Gossip flew round and round about Elizabeth, but that did not deter her next suitor, Willis Routt. He married her in 1858 and soon followed her earlier husbands to the cemetery.

Elizabeth then converted her home into a tavern for mule drovers. It was located on the old road to Nashville. She became involved in a quarrel with a neighbor, Abner Tate, and persuaded her next suitor, D. H. Bingham, to charge Tate with murder.

Tate published a defense in which he alleged that Mrs. Routt's bridal chamber was "a charnal house" and that "she was a woman around whose marriage couch six grinning skeletons were already hung."

Mrs. Routt retaliated with a suit for $50,000, charging defamation of character. Public opinion rendered the only decision in the case, and Mrs. Routt sold her house and left the state.

Old Adam Dale, who had settled in DeKalb County in 1797, died in Hazel Green in 1851, and presumably he had been living in his daughter's house. The *Alabama Guide Book* says he is buried in the family plot, but Hale's reliable history of DeKalb County says surviving children moved his body to Columbia, Tennessee, after his wife's death, perhaps leaving his marker at Hazel Green.

Whatever happened on the old mound where Indian fires once burned, Elizabeth Dale made a reputation that survives today. Residents say there are stories that seven men's hats, all belonging to departed husbands, hang in the closet.

Where did that seventh hat come from? They don't say.

WILLIAMSON COUNTY:
A Knob and a Beech Tree

Roper's Knob

Green hills, the winding Harpeth, a great battlefield, and a consciousness of history—these are a part of the heritage of Williamson County. The most famous natural landmark of the region is Roper's Knob, just north of Franklin.

The late James E. Caldwell, who would become one of Nashville's wealthiest citizens in the years after 1900, came to this region as a boy. In his *Recollections of a Lifetime* he described what he found.

"We reached Franklin about the Fourth of July, 1876, going to the Rosser Place on the Nashville Pike about a mile and a half from town, where Spencer's Creek crosses the road. The house still stands. It was at that time new and fresh, with some fifty or sixty acres of land connected with it. . . .

"Roper's Knob and Shute's Knob, those Siamese twin sentinels, standing out in bold relief, overlooking the Harpeth River Valley, towered right up at the back of the house.

"My mother never complained or made any reference to our poverty, which at that time clearly reached its height.

"Nowhere on earth are there kinder, better, or nicer people than in and around Franklin. Just in sight of us lived the Campbells and the Ewings. There were three Campbell boys—and two Ewing boys likewise.

"We all went to Mr. McNutt's private school. He had one

7

assistant, Mr. Binford. There were eighty scholars in all, and these two men did all the teaching.

"Baseball had never been played at Franklin, and so my brother and I introduced it there, and the rival schools—McNutt's and Campbell's—had great sport with each other.

"That winter was very rough and cold. We had had rather a long spell, and so the woodpile was about exhausted before I ventured out with the horse and cart upon the cold, bleak sides of Roper's Knob for wood; then finally it had to be done.

"Out and up I went, the road carrying me around to the north side of the hill, and the wood was only to be had very near the top. It seemed to me that wind would cut me in two, but I got my load and started down.

"The ground was frozen hard and covered more or less with ice and snow, and the wind was blowing a perfect gale. I had gone but a little distance when, in crossing a slippery, shelving rock, the cart slid off the edge and broke one of the wheels, and so cart and wood spilled out down the side of the hill.

"Fortunately, I was walking and driving to keep as warm as possible, and so avoided any personal injury, but when I stood there upon that bleak, desolate hillside, with the temperature at zero, snow and ice underfoot, and the wind cutting my face and hands like a knife; as I say, when I stood there and looked down at that house with no wood and out upon that great desert of frozen landscape, all the beauty and grandeur went out of it, and perfect terror seized upon me, and the thought flashed through my mind—'Must we all freeze to death and perish utterly?'

"Then the blood of my Scotch ancestors, who no doubt had for generation after generation faced just such conditions on the mountainsides of Scotland, came to my rescue.

"I summoned up my courage, looked out on that forlorn prospect, and soliloquized that there must be some way out and that there must be better conditions to be had somewhere in the world, and I resolved then and there to find them.

"I verily believe that was the great event in my life and proved an everlasting spur to action and fixed determination TO SAVE, as affording the sure road to better living. That impulse has never left me—it became a fixed habit for life. I borrowed a cart, got that wood down off that hillside, and never let that woodpile get low again and never have allowed such want to get that close to me since."

So history was made on Roper's Knob that day—at least in the life of one man and his family.

One observer of Franklin's recent growth and progress says that James E. Caldwell's son, Rogers, deserves a share of the credit. Rogers Caldwell died in 1968 after living for several years on Bridge Avenue in Franklin.

"By the force of his personality, by his kindliness and his interest in people," this observer said, "Rogers Caldwell influenced real estate men to do what was best for the community. He was a positive force in the town."

So perhaps the effect of that winter scene on Roper's Knob is still felt in Franklin.

A Giant Beech Tree

George Washington Herbert died in 1968 at his farm on the old Smyrna Road in the edge of Williamson County. He had lived long on the land and had a feeling for trees, livestock, and pasture. In a narrow valley on his farm a beech forest once stood, through which, it is believed, a buffalo trail had passed. Indians had passed that way, and just a few miles away was the site of an ancient Indian village.

In years gone by it was a custom for people to cut their initials and a date on beech trees. The early settlers, especially, made marks on bark. Daniel Boone's beech tree where he "kiled a bar" is an example.

The place where the initials are carved in the bark will not grow higher from the ground. The slit in the bark will expand with the growth of the tree and trunk and grow larger as the tree grows.

One giant beech tree is still standing in the narrow valley, and a state forester said it could be over four hundred years old. This beech tree had many names and dates, including one

from the Overton family. But one name, near the ground, was
so old and grown with the years it could not be read. It appeared
to be a French name, with the prefix "la" or "de." But the
date, in old-fashioned numbers, was plain—1563. Before many
more years, this landmark of the centuries will be gone.

*1563—an early date that is still visible on
a giant beech tree in Williamson County.*

LOST CREEK VALLEY

According to the *Tennessee Gazetteer* of 1834, " 'Lost Creek is a branch of Caney Fork in White County. Upon this creek are extensive falls, some of them thirty feet in perpendicular height. It affords sufficient water to propel machinery about half the year and is about ten miles in length. And nature, after exhibiting much variety in the romantic appearance of its falls and the impetuosity of its current, has, as if weary of its passage, directed its course to the foot of a stupendous mountain, where the stream is ingulphed and lost in the silent grandeur of the surrounding objects.'—Haywood."

Judge John Haywood, who lived at Tusculum out on Nolensville Road, was a giant jurist and the first historian of Tennessee. He loved adjectives, thus his descriptions were sometimes exaggerated, but his *Natural and Aboriginal History of Tennessee,* published in 1823, is one of the most valuable and sought after books ever published in the state.

In *Resources of Tennessee,* Killebrew wrote:
"At about half the height of the Cumberland Table Land is the terrace or 'bench.' This terrace has the same elevation as the tables or tops of most of the little mountains, or outliers. It affords sites for some beautiful farms and orchards. . . . The valley of Lost Creek, cut off and completely encompassed by Pine Mountain, an arm of the Cumberland, is on a level with the terrace. . . .
"In the elevated valley of Lost Creek are a number of beautiful

11

farms, where the people dwell, retired and caring little for the changes that agitate the world abroad. The waters of the creek linger lovingly in the Arcadian retreat, protracting their stay by many graceful meanders, and then steal away through an underground channel beneath the mountains into the Caney Fork."

A road passes through a gap in Pine Mountain to the elevated valley of Lost Creek. The "breaks in the mountain" mark the border of Lost Creek Valley. This place could be called the "valley of the old folks." Everybody farms, and the average age of the people is more than sixty-five. Many are around eighty. There are fifty-two people living in the valley on sixteen farms. Many of these farms include high land on the mountain which is covered with salable timber. The bottom land averages about a hundred acres for each farm. Both limestone and sandstone soil are found in the valley, with the sandy soil on the plateau. It is not as rich as the bottom land but is looser, more easily worked, and responds well to fertilizers.

The average farm in Lost Creek Valley is worth, with its equipment, about $30,000. With one possible exception, not a farm in the valley is mortgaged. The average farm has a potential of earning about $4,000 a year, but most of them produce no more than half as much in cash or its equivalent.

Thirty years ago the valley had a community school and a general store. Both are long since gone. There are two churches, the Church of Christ and the Presbyterian-Methodist church.

Lost Creek makes several descents into the earth. At the very end of the valley, backed up against Pine Mountain, is a beetling limestone rock where one can look down through the trees and undergrowth at the hurrying waters of the creek as they disappear into the base of the mountain.

The gorge where the creek disappears is steep, wooded, and infested with copperheads. But about a mile down the road, on the far side of the mountain, the hillside is clear, and a rocky stream bed leads to the wild, splashing, seventy-foot falls of

The hidden seventy-foot falls of Lost Creek.

Lost Creek. Few people have seen this spectacular waterfall in this almost inaccessible spot, but it's well worth all the trouble.

Lost Creek Valley is indeed a secluded and sheltered community, but its past and present are a valid part of the American

scene. On the wall of one home hangs a big blue and white
platter showing the landing of Lafayette in America in 1824—the
year before he made his historic visit to Nashville. The same
platter is treasured elsewhere—even in museums. But in this
"Valley of the Old Folks" it hangs on the wall of a farm home,
as much a part of America as the hills, creeks, and waterfalls
that mark the rural scene.

*One of the bridges which crosses Lost Creek,
a branch of Caney Fork, in White County.*

CARTHAGE AND TWO RIVERS

The old road to Carthage comes in north of the Cumberland, through Dixon Springs. Perhaps it is the most beautiful approach to the town, and it has never been better described than by the young English traveler, Francis Baily, who passed that way in 1797.

"Started by daylight," wrote Baily, "and proceeded on to the ferry. When I came to within two miles of the place I was brought to the brow of the highlands. From this spot I had a most delightful view of the surrounding country, and of the distant hills which border upon the Cumberland, presenting a wild, mountainous appearance which could not fail to interest the spectator.

"Having descended into the bottom, I passed one or two habitations and at last came to the ferryhouse where I stopped. Giving my horse some corn, I took breakfast with my host, who furnished me with some coffee and some fried rashers of bacon, served up with Indian bread—a common breakfast in this part of the country.

"A little distance below the house a stream called the Caney Fork comes in . . . so called from the cane brakes on its banks."

Baily's host was William Walton, farmer, ferryman, and builder of the road east across the mountain. Walton was the first settler on the present site of Carthage.

Carthage is on one side of the river while on the other side is the rocky face of a towering bluff. The bluff overlooks the Cordell Hull bridge, which spans the Cumberland and links Carthage to the east-west highways.

15

The old Myer Bridge which once crossed the Cumberland at
Carthage. Photo courtesy the Carthage Courier.

The river, high hills, and rock-faced bluff are not the only Carthage attractions. The Cordell Hull Bridge is a thing of beauty, but its predecessor, a privately owned toll bridge, was even more famous.

It was built between 1906 and 1908 for W. E. Myer and "Wint" Williams and was long a useful landmark at Carthage. Andy Reed of the Carthage *Courier* says tolls ranged from a nickel for a person walking to twenty cents for a loaded wagon and team. The last span on the old bridge was pulled down on May 26, 1936. Reed reported that hundreds of saddened Smith countians stood on the banks of the Cumberland to watch the old bridge go.

Mrs. Andy Reed, Jr., of Carthage wrote of the old bridge:

"I remember how slender and fragile it looked. I have stood on it many times, watching until I was dizzy the heavy drift flowing in the swift current of the muddy, flooded Cumberland."

A story is told that long ago a traveling circus, expecting

to make a one-day stand in Carthage, brought its animals to the bridge only to find that the toll keeper wanted five dollars for each elephant to cross over. Whereupon the circus man, pleading poverty, fell on his knees and said, "For the love of God, Mr. Myer, let them elephants pass."

But Myer would not. So the circus was held south of the river, and the people paid to go across and see it!

The Cumberland at Carthage has all the beauty of the Tennessee at Chattanooga, though not on so grand a scale. But the Cumberland has the added attraction of the Caney Fork, its largest tributary, curving up from the south through the green knobs of the Highland Rim. Breaking out of the hills into the wide valley of the Cumberland the once turbulent Caney, now smooth as a mill pond, curves gently to the west and glides into the Cumberland like a kitten coming home.

An early historian wrote that along the Caney Fork the first settlers ran into heavy cane brakes that made travel almost impossible. "Because of the danger of piercing the horses' legs if cut low, they determined to cut off the leafy, heavy tops, and then press their teams and wagons over them."—S. M. Fite.

It was on the Caney Fork in 1792 that Sumner County's Lieutenant William Snoddy battled Indians at the Rock Island fort. Here now stands the Great Falls Dam, an early power installation that served the Tennessee Electric Power Company and is now a part of TVA's power supply. Farther down stream is the great Center Hill Dam, built without a lock, twenty-six miles above Carthage. The new Hull Dam on the Cumberland does have a lock and makes the river navigable for many miles upstream.

Near the point where Walton put Baily ashore is the old ferryboat landing. When he stood on this narrow tongue of land Baily wrote:

"I was landed exactly on the point of land where the two rivers met. The prospect from the middle of the stream was delightful; you appeared to be in the center of three grand rivers, whose banks were everywhere formed of lofty eminences, towering over each other with a kind of majestic pride, and covered with verdure to their very summits."

Swinging south in a sweeping curve the stream is sometimes less than paddle deep. Overlooking the river is the marble home of Senator Albert Gore and his wife, Pauline. The Gore farm extends for perhaps half a mile along the right bank. On the other side of the stream is level soil intervened with rocky bluffs.

Smith County was named for General Daniel Smith, surveyor and man of affairs, whose descendants still live on his Revolutionary grant in Sumner County. It is generally believed Carthage was named by General James Winchester.

Smith County has had some famous citizens, going all the way back to early settlers Moses Fisk, an educator, and Joe Bishop, a rough and tumble hunter and scout who might be described as Fisk's opposite number.

It's not too hard to get an argument in Carthage. One man said the Hull Dam would provide flood control, another said it wouldn't, and another volunteered the opinion that Cordell Hull was a great statesman, but he "never did anything for Carthage."

Be that as it may, the bridge is named for the man Franklin Roosevelt called the Gray Eagle. The dam is named for him, and a painting of Hull by a sister-in-law of Senator Gore hangs in the public library.

VALLEY OF THE WOLF

It's a long way to Tipperary,
It's a long way to go . . .

Alvin York had always wanted "a piece of bottom land," and he finally got it. And ten miles from Jamestown, named for James Fentress, a statesman before the Civil War, is the Valley of the Three Forks of the Wolf. Here three streams, each with a valley of its own, unite to make beautiful bottom land three miles wide. Main Fork, Middle Fork, and Rottin Fork join here to become the Wolf River.

In the heart of this green valley is the big yellow frame home of Sergeant Alvin C. York.

There's a rose that grows in No-Man's Land,
And 'tis wonderful to see . . .

Like the speaker who "needs no introduction," York's story is seldom told any more, but the incident that made him great is worth repeating.

As a bachelor of twenty-nine, Alvin York was a tough mountaineer, hunter, and blacksmith, who got caught in the draft of 1917. Two years before he had gotten religion because of the teaching of Pastor Pile, who preached and ran the post office and grocery store at Pall Mall. York gave up smoking, drinking, and cussing and spent much time reading the Bible. He joined the Church of Christ in Christian Union and was known as the "Singing Elder."

19

York was a conscientious objector, so he, with the help of Pastor Pile, tried in vain to stay out of the army. He would have gotten a discharge not long after being drafted had he not decided to fight. He reached his decision while home on a furlough sitting under the brow of Cumberland Mountain reading his Bible.

York was in Company G of the 328th Battalion of the 82nd Division, now the famous 82nd Airborne. After reaching the front in France, his outfit participated in the St. Mihiel offensive and the Battle of Argonne Forest.

K-K-K Katie, beautiful Katie,
You're the only G-G-G Girl that I adore . . .

On October 8, 1918, at Chateau Thierry, Company G was engaged in heavy fighting on the road from Varennes to Fleville. "And oh, my!" York wrote in his diary. "The dead were all along the road, and their mouths were open and their eyes, too, but they couldn't see nothing no more nohow. And it was wet and cold and damp."

In a little valley the battalion was pinned down by German machine gun fire from a high ridge. On the left a support platoon, commanded by Sergeant Harry Parsons, was ordered to flank the machine gunners and silence them. York was a corporal in this platoon. The platoon was ordinarily armed with French "sho-sho" guns (automatic rifles), but this time it was armed with Enfield rifles, Colt .45 automatic pistols, and a few "potato mashers" (grenades).

Two squads, seventeen men in all, flanked the Germans and came up in rear of the second line. They surprised about seventy-five Germans in a headquarters conference and captured them all, firing only a few shots. Only one of the Germans, a major, was armed.

Just at this point the German machine gunners in the front line, seeing what was happening in their rear, turned their guns on the Americans, killing six and wounding three, including all the noncoms except York. He was in command. The other survivors guarded the prisoners and took whatever cover they could find.

York, caught in the open, fired his rifle until his clips were exhausted, and then used his pistol. "Every time one showed his head," he said, "I teched him off."

Six Germans charged York with bayonets, and he picked them off, shooting the last man first. After he had personally accounted for twenty-five Germans, the major he had captured persuaded the others to surrender. York then led his seven remaining men and prisoners through the German front line, taking more prisoners as he went. In all he took 132 prisoners back to the American lines, and the three wounded Americans also reached their own lines safely.

Marshal Foch called York's battle "the greatest thing accomplished by any private soldier of all the armies of Europe." General Pershing called him "the outstanding civilian soldier of the war." He was awarded the Medal of Honor, the French Legion of Honour, the Croix de Guerre with palms, the Italian War Cross, the Medaille Militaire, and the Tennessee Medal for Valor.

> *Over there . . . over there . . .*
> *Send the word . . . over there . . .*

In May, 1919, the sergeant was given a hero's welcome in Washington and New York. His home state voted him the beautiful medal set in diamonds and sapphires, and the Nashville Rotary Club helped him acquire his farm in the bottom land of the Three Forks of the Wolf. Practically half the state attended his wedding to Miss Gracie, his boyhood sweetheart.

The red-headed sergeant never did settle down. Things were always happening to him. People came to write books and stories about him. He wrote a column for *The Nashville Tennessean*. He labored to fund a mountain vocational school, York Institute, at Jamestown. He prevailed on the government to build a road across the plateau, and today it is called by his name.

Sergeant York was the subject of a major motion picture; he found an oil well on his farm; he made patriotic speeches;

*Sergeant Alvin
York and his
mother after his
return from World
War I.*

he raised money for the school and got embroiled in arguments
with school officials about the institute and with the federal
government about his taxes.

"I know," York is quoted by his biographer, Skeyhill, "that
I am a tolable good shot. But I don't care how good a shot
a man is, hit ain't in the nature of things for one man with
an army rifle and a pistol to whip thirty-five machine guns that
can each fire over six hundred shots a minute, from a pin't
blank range of between twenty and thirty yards. . . . And I'm
a-telling you the hand of God must have been in that fight."

Some people are cynical about York's military achievement,
saying that "the Germans were ready to surrender anyway."
But York did not brag; his record speaks for itself. By character,
inheritance, and experience, he was a man fitted to do the thing
he did. He had the job to do, and he did it.

RUGBY:
A Noble Experiment

The story of Rugby is the story of a "noble experiment" that failed. But it was a grand failure, and despite the failure, the traditions and ghosts and the long, lost laughter of a more prosperous and happy time still make Rugby an interesting and romantic spot.

In the decade after the American Civil War, Thomas Hughes, English novelist, earned a fortune with his *Tom Brown's School Days* and other Tom Brown books. This good, generous man, wishing to help the ne'er-do-well "younger sons" of English noblemen, decided to build what he called a "castle in Spain." Hughes "castle" took the form of an English settlement at what was later Rugby—previously called Plateau City—on Cumberland Mountain.

Land on the plateau was cheap. Unimproved, it was selling at from fifty cents to one dollar an acre in 1874. In 1877 a group of Boston businessmen founded Plateau City. It never got off the ground, and the Bostonians were at the end of their rope when the English group, headed by the wealthy novelist, took over.

The "Board of Aid to Land Ownership" laid out streets, built homes for Hughes and other settlers, a guest house, a hotel, a school, a church, and a library. The young gentlemen came, and the first thing they did was build a tennis court. The mountaineers were aghast at such doings.

The settlement was to be a "wedding" of the best of England and America, and for a year or two it flourished. Thomas Hughes

23

remained for a while; his mother is buried at Rugby. But a typhoid epidemic, during a great drought on the plateau, took the lives of many of the young settlers. Most of them were unused to labor, and the upland soil yielded but scanty crops from their amateurish efforts at farming.

One young settler, having been persuaded to do a day's work for someone else, was paid a dollar. This he framed. "It is the first and last," he said, "that I will ever earn in that manner."

Hughes returned to England, having suffered heavy financial losses, and many of the young Englishmen followed his example. Only a few of the original settlers remained. But the young Englishmen at Rugby "builded better than they knew." They left behind a tradition of culture and gentility that is remembered in Rugby today. The school and the hotel have long since gone up in smoke. But the library remains—and such a library! It is like walking into another generation.

The beautiful little library at Rugby.

The little library still looks just as it did when it was dedicated and named for Thomas Hughes in 1882. There are no lights—except the sunlight that falls through the tall, narrow windows when the shutters are opened and a kerosene lamp.

There are pictures of Thomas Hughes and other "colonists" on the walls, and the tables, desks, and chairs are just as the young gentlemen left them three quarters of a century ago. There is a wonderful collection of children's books of the period and some beautiful facsimile reproductions of drawings from Charles Dickens.

The Episcopal church, built by the Englishmen, has been cared for by the Diocese of Tennessee, and time has only mellowed the building and made it more beautiful. Inside everything is just as it was long ago, including the organ made in London and a beautiful stained-glass window dedicated to Mary Blacklock and Margaret Hughes, mother of the novelist.

Christ Episcopal Church at Rugby, established in 1880. Photo courtesy of Tennessee Conservation Department.

The Newbury House, the original Rugby guest house, is completely furnished but has not been lived in for half a century, except for a few weeks in the summer. It contains many beautiful antiques, and it, too, is like walking into yesterday.

Rugby, which lies between the steep valleys of the Clear Fork and White Oak rivers that unite near the town to form the Great South Fork of the Cumberland, is not related to the pioneer beginnings of Tennessee. But it is rich in the history of the Victorian period. The files of three newspapers, published during its heyday, tell a romantic and stirring story of a dream that was finally smothered by the harsh realities of plateau farming in the days when there were no county agents.

In front of the little church one can almost hear the voice of a young Englishman as he complained after a service one Sunday:

"They prayed for the president, but they said not a word about Queen Vic!"

Slowly the Rugby buildings, all made of wood, are weathering and rotting. Maybe some day, before it is too late, a way will be found to save the church, the library, the Newbury house, and perhaps other original buildings.

RIVER OF RAISINS:
Disaster in a Frozen Land

"Remember the Raisin" is a famous battle cry of American history, but over the long years since 1813 Americans have forgotten the Raisin. Perhaps they wanted to forget.

Frenchtown, where the Battle of the Raisin was fought, has changed its name since that tragic day. Now it is Monroe, Michigan, a town of approximately twenty thousand people, most of whom have never heard of General James Winchester of Tennessee and his doomed army of Kentuckians.

The truth is that the Indians won at the Raisin. In snow, ice, fire, and smoke, the little army of Kentuckians dissolved in its own blood.

Murder and massacre followed defeat, and to this day the name of British Colonel Henry Proctor—where it is recorded or remembered in this country—is associated with villainy.

There was heroism at the Raisin, but the scene there had nothing to do with the storybook side of war. An officer in the enemy army of British and Indians described the Kentuckians captured at the Raisin:

"The appearance of the American prisoners captured at Frenchtown was miserable to the last degree. They had the air of men to whom cleanliness was a virtue unknown, and their squalid bodies were covered by habiliments that had evidently undergone every change of season, and were arrived at the last stage of repair. It was the depth of winter, but scarcely an individual was in possession of a greatcoat or cloak, and few of them wore garments of wool of any description.

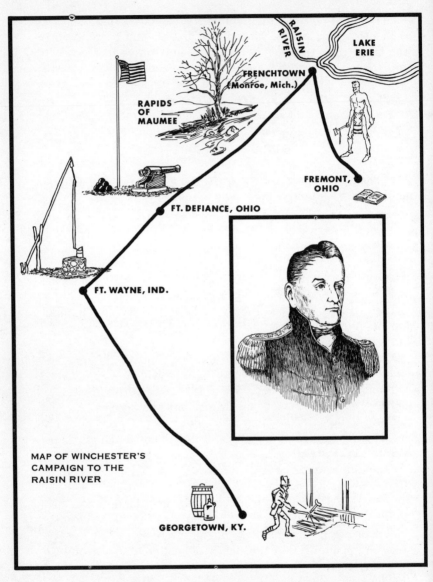

RAISIN RIVER

LAKE ERIE

FRENCHTOWN
(Monroe, Mich.)

RAPIDS OF MAUMEE

FREMONT, OHIO

FT. DEFIANCE, OHIO

FT. WAYNE, IND.

MAP OF WINCHESTER'S
CAMPAIGN TO THE
RAISIN RIVER

GEORGETOWN, KY.

*Map of the trip to the River of Raisins, with
inset drawing of General James Winchester.*

"They still retained their summer dress, consisting of cotton stuff of various colors, shaped into frocks, and descending to the knee; their trousers were of the same material. They were covered with slouch hats, worn bare by constant use, beneath which their long hair fell matted and uncombed over their cheeks."

Translating these words into time and place—In the deep cold of a northern winter, sick and hungry, on short rations or no rations, exhausted by the labor of pulling their wounded over snow and ice, and still wearing tattered summer clothing, these men went into battle against well-equipped British regulars and Indians who were native to the country and inured to its hardships.

Washington's men at Valley Forge during the Revolution, Confederate troops barefoot in the hills at Nashville in 1864— these are famous examples of the sufferings of American troops in wartime. But surely no army ever suffered more than this one.

"The half of what was endured has never yet been published to the world," wrote Kentucky soldier William Atherton, "and perhaps never will."

For General Winchester it had all started on Bledsoe's Creek in Middle Tennessee in the warm spring of 1812. There the general lived in his great stone house, Cragfont, with its rose garden, wine cellar, and well-stocked smokehouse. Seven six-pointed iron stars adorned the front of the general's house; but so far as his military career was concerned, they were not lucky stars.

A veteran of the Revolution and the Indian wars, the general had a reputation as a fearless leader. His military experience included campaigns as a regular army officer and as an officer of the Tennessee militia. He had the confidence of his neighbors, including Andrew Jackson. But he had been a prisoner of the British during the Revolution, and his luck was to be no better in the War of 1812.

The general was an active, imaginative man of distinguished ancestry and considerable intellectual attainments. He is credited with giving classical names to such Tennessee towns and cities as Memphis, Rome, Carthage, and Cairo. In the spring of 1812, as war with Britain neared, he was commissioned a brigadier general in the United States Army. He immediately went to Lexington, Kentucky, and began raising troops for the defense of the Northwest.

Some historians have commented that many years had passed since Winchester's Revolutionary and Indian battles, that he had been living in elegance and ease, and at sixty he was hardly the man to lead a campaign into the northern woods.

But the general believed in physical fitness. He kept up with the army—sometimes ahead of it—and apparently suffered no more from rigors of the march than did younger men. However, the Kentucky militiamen resented the leadership of Winchester—a regular army man. They wanted William Henry Harrison, hero of the victory over the Indians at the 1811 Battle of Tippecanoe, to be their commander.

In the continuing hassle over the command Winchester and Harrison handled themselves well, but discontent of the militiamen may have been a factor in the disaster that was to follow.

As the army of Kentuckians was building in the late summer of 1812, patriotism flamed high. At Frankfort old Governor Charles Scott reviewed Captain Paschal Hickman's company from Franklin County. Orlando Brown, wrote:

"The soldiers were drawn up in a line between the front steps and the fence, and servants were busy going from man to man, one bearing a pail full of whiskey and the other a pail of water.

"The governor was hobbling along on his crutch with his gray hair streaming in the wind and tears running down his aged cheeks, taking his final leave, wishing them God speed, and conjuring them to be brave. Some time before this the governor had fallen on the slick steps of the house, from the effects of which he was ever after lame, and had to use a crutch.

"By the time he had gone the rounds of the company his emotion had become almost too big for speech, and turning abruptly towards the steps, he wore his crutch out on them, explaining with every blow—'If it hadn't been for you, I could have gone with the boys myself!' "

At Georgetown the army was paraded and addressed by Henry

Clay, then speaker of the U. S. House of Representatives. Clay
spoke "with his usual eloquence."

On that very day, unknown to Clay and the soldiers, the
American General William Hull was surrendering Detroit to
the British and Indians without a fight. The Kentuckians were
expecting to cooperate with Hull's army to conquer upper Canada. "How much at variance," wrote the historian McAfee, "the
treacherous, dastardly deeds of the general and the animating,
patriotic anticipations of the orator!"

The men had been promised sixteen dollars in lieu of clothing
they had not received, but the money was not paid. They were
advised by the officers to go without and trust to the justice
of the government, or return home. Six men decided to go home,
and they were drummed out of camp.

"This was a disgrace," noted McAfee, "which no man of any
honor or feeling could have endured. When they arrived at home,
some of them were treated with so much contempt by their
wives, that they returned to the army and continued to discharge
their duty."

The American surrender of Detroit had put the whole Northwest in danger. General Harrison, who soon received command
of the troops in that region, recognized that Fort Wayne, unless
it could be relieved, would fall to the British and their Indian
allies. Judge John H. DeWitt, in the *Tennessee Historical Magazine,* described problems facing the Americans.

"In 1812 the country comprising the present states of Ohio,
Indiana, Illinois, and Michigan was thinly settled except eastern
Ohio and southern Indiana. Much of it was a wilderness, with
occasional roads swampy and almost impassable in winter. It
was occupied by the Indian tribes dominated by Tecumseh,
which had been overcome in 1811 by the Americans under
William Henry Harrison at the Battle of Tippecanoe. Michigan
was a territory with less than five thousand inhabitants.

"Across the river from Detroit, in upper Canada, the British
erected fortifications, and near the mouth of the Detroit River,
just above Lake Erie, they held Fort Malden. Early in 1812
it became evident they were preparing for an invasion of the
United States."

The army took the "Dry Ridge Road" to Cincinnati. The old road is still there, narrow, meandering, and lonely—almost deserted in favor of the new superhighway running parallel. North of the Ohio River, along Highway 127, lies the western border of the state. This is corn country, with beautiful farm homes and rich black soil—a far cry from the desolate swamps and woodland that greeted the little band of Kentuckians in 1812.

As the army approached Fort Wayne a soldier wrote:

" 'Tis almost impossible to travel through the woods in the vicinity of Fort Wayne, the stench arising from the hogs and cattle being so great. The Indians were busy firing on the fort for two days previous to our arrival."

At Fort Wayne General Winchester took command of the Northwestern army, and General Harrison moved south to collect more troops. Late in September Winchester moved his force north and eastward fifty miles to Fort Defiance, now Defiance, Ohio, at the junction of the Maumee and Auglaize rivers.

"He was in the heart of the wilderness," wrote Judge DeWitt, "with scarcely any roads and Indians lurking on the line of march."

An American flag, historical markers, and a cannon today mark the spot near the public library in Defiance, Ohio. A few yards up the Auglaize from the confluence of the rivers, Winchester and his men built Fort Winchester.

Cold winter winds whip over the site now, snapping the Stars and Stripes on its staff. A sign on the bank of the Auglaize wrongly credits Harrison with building Fort Winchester—but the general did pick the site for the fortification.

The famished troops were on the verge of mutiny—but Harrison arrived in the nick of time to pacify them. His efforts were aided by the fact that he brought with him several pack-horses loaded with flour. Harrison was now a major general in command of the Northwestern forces, but he persuaded Winchester to take command of the left wing at the fort, and Harrison returned to St. Mary's, Ohio.

Winchester's command now consisted of a detachment of the

17th U. S. Regiment under Colonel Samuel Wells, a detachment of the 14th U. S. Regiment, and regiments of Kentucky troops commanded by Colonels Scott, Jennings, Pogue, Lewis, Barbee, and Allen.

As Christmas came the cold deepened, and DeWitt noted that "fevers and other diseases raged in almost every tent. The great trouble lay in the feeble support given by the War Department."

Just south of Toledo the Maumee River swirls through rocks and shoals. Winchester was now ordered to move his eleven hundred men to this "Rapids," where he was promised provisions and support.

"We are now commencing," wrote soldier Elias Darnell, "one of the most serious marches ever performed by the Americans."

Winchester ordered the men to make sleds to carry provisions, but the historian Clift noted that "even as the men built these crude vehicles they realized there was not in the whole camp a horse capable of pulling even an empty sled." Clift commented that it was "now or never for General Winchester. His men had suffered all that soldiers could be called upon to suffer."

Over frozen streams and through two-foot snow the men pulled the sleds, and after eleven days they arrived at the Rapids. It was almost the middle of January.

On January 13 two Frenchmen arrived in the Kentucky camp from Frenchtown, thirty-eight miles to the north on the Raisin River, called by the French La Riviere aux Raisins. The Indians, they said, were collecting with the British around Frenchtown and were threatening to burn the village. They implored Winchester and his army for help.

Other messengers came in pleading for their defenseless people, saying the Indians were threatening to murder families and burn their homes. Still another messenger said the enemy was five hundred strong and being reinforced.

"To advance would be difficult," wrote Judge DeWitt, "but the call of humanity required it."

General Winchester's defense of his advance to the Raisin to help the beleaguered citizens there is a classic of American history. It reads:

"The arms of the United States are as irrevocably bound to protect a single individual as a million. The social compact becomes a rope of sand, is rent asunder, the instant a single individual is sacrificed without his assent, even for the salvation of the republic."

The American commander sent Colonels Lewis and Allen, with 450 men to the Raisin, where they arrived on January 18. Charging across the frozen river they drove off a force of British and Indians equal to their own. Two days later Winchester, with 250 men, arrived on the Raisin. The river was a solid sheet of ice, and the general elected to spend the night on the south side, half a mile from his battle line.

The American officers were uneasy. Reinforcements did not appear—they would be too late. Some accounts indicate Winchester expected an attack, others that he was taken by surprise.

The weather was bitter cold, but the men had apples and cider, along with flour and a ton of beef captured on the 18th in the first Battle of the Raisin.

On the 19th the troops had collected their dead from the first battle. "All the men found—thirteen in number—were scalped and stripped of their clothing, their bodies frozen stiff."

The little army was now disposed on the north bank of the Raisin, where most of the village lay. On the night of January 21, the force numbered fewer than a thousand, with eight hundred on the north bank.

About six hundred of these had some protection behind a picket fence. On the right, 250 regulars under Colonel Samuel Wells were camped in an open field.

Wells had contrived to be sent back to the Rapids as a courier. Winchester told Wells (according to Thomas Dudley) that "if you are disposed to leave your command in the immediate vicinity of the enemy, when a battle is certain, you can go." Wells went. If this report is correct, Winchester was not surprised by the attack at the Raisin.

As the drums beat reveille in the half-light of morning, Proctor struck. He had a body of five hundred troops and militia, eight hundred Indians under Roundhead, a Huron chief, and three light field pieces. This force had marched two days from the

British fort at Malden, and spent the night of the 21st within five miles of the American position.

The historian Clift wrote:

"The British and Indians were advancing in attack formation as the rattling of drums called the Americans to wakefulness. Listening to the drums, alone in the mist, the American sentry did not hear the enemy until reveille had finished and the rumble of enemy gun carriages loomed before him.

"The Kentuckians drew first blood. The sentry turned and fired and hit Gates, the leading grenadier of the 41st, right through the head. The ball went in one ear and out the other."

Behind the picket fence the Kentucky militia stemmed the attack, the men firing their rifles with deadly effect. But on the right the unprotected regulars caved in under flanking attack by the Indians.

Winchester, arriving on the line without his uniform coat, tried to rally these men. The brave militiamen leaped from behind their barricade to help the men on the right. The attempt was a bloody failure.

The Jessamine County Blues were sent out to bring in the wounded and discovered that the Indians had practically surrounded the town. The men retreated into a small sunken lane which proved a death trap, as the fire from the hidden Indians cut them to pieces. Colonel John Allen used his sword in a last sweeping stroke to kill an Indian, and another standing near shot him dead.

On the right side of the American line the retreat toward the stockade became a route. Unable to reach the shelter of the pickets, the men ran toward the frozen river. A group of twenty men was cut down by the Indians after they had "grounded their arms" in an attempt to surrender. The tomahawks of the Indians had their quota of blood and scalps.

General Winchester was among those captured by Indians under Roundhead. Taken before Proctor, he was advised that Americans within the stockade were still holding out.

Proctor intimated that if he had to storm the stockade, the town would be burned and prisoners turned over to the Indians. On the other hand, if Americans surrendered, he would accept

responsibility for the lives of the prisoners and the conduct of
the Indians.

Winchester then "recommended" surrender to the officer next
in command, and the defeat of his little army was complete.
Proctor immediately broke his word. Prisoners the Indians had
taken were left in their hands and driven from the village, hands
tied behind their backs. One of these was William Atherton
of Shelby County, Kentucky, who afterwards put his experiences
in a book, *Narrative of the Suffering and Defeat of the North-
Western Army Under General Winchester.*

The British regulars, supposing General Harrison to be in
the neighborhood with a large force, pulled out for Malden on
the afternoon of January 22, the day of the battle. The next
day, the British promised, sleds would be sent to take the
wounded to Malden.

No sleds came. Instead, hundreds of skulking Indians descended on the helpless town. By ten o'clock perhaps two
hundred of them headed for the houses where the wounded
were watching their every move.

By the testimony of a reputable witness, the Indians were
not drunk. They systematically robbed the wounded, murdered
them, scalped them, and stripped them of their clothes. Two
houses were burned, with forty-nine wounded men inside. Those
who could crawl to the doors were tomahawked as they came
out. The rest were burned to death in the flames.

Dr. Gustavus Bower described the murder of Charles Sears:
"The Indian raised his tomahawk and struck him on the
shoulder, which cut into the cavity of the body. Sears then
caught hold of the tomahawk and appeared to resist, and upon
my telling him that his fate was inevitable, he closed his eyes
and received the savage blow which terminated his existence.
I was near enough to receive the brains and blood on my blanket."

William Atherton wrote: "I saw a striking example of the
estimate a man places on life. I saw some of our own company—
old acquaintances who were so badly wounded they could
scarcely be moved in their beds, understanding that those who

could not travel on foot to Malden were all to be tomahawked, pass on their way to Malden, hobbling along on sticks. Poor fellows, they were soon overtaken by their merciless enemies and inhumanly butchered."

About sixty or sixty-five men were thus murdered, among them men who had been prominent in the pioneer life of Kentucky. The Kentucky historical marker at Georgetown says Winchester had 1,050 men, and all but thirty were killed, massacred, wounded, or captured.

Nine Kentucky counties not yet formed were named for men who died. They are Allen, Ballard, Graves, Hart, Hickman, Edmondson, McCracken, Meade, and Simpson.

As for Proctor, Winchester could hardly find words to express his opinion:

"The English language does not afford epithets sufficiently powerful or descriptive. . . . I find it in vain to appeal to a man whose trade is rapine, and whose bread is murder."

General Winchester survived his captivity, and later fought under Jackson in the southern theater of the war. As events turned out it was Jackson, victor at New Orleans, who eclipsed Harrison as the national hero.

After the war Winchester defended his military conduct in his restrained and beautifully written *Historical Details* of the campaign, published at Lexington, Kentucky, in 1818. Not more than half a dozen copies of this little book exist in America, and apparently none in Kentucky and Tennessee.

Harrison and the Kentuckians had another shot at Proctor and the Indians. It came on the Thames River, in October 1813. The historian Clift wrote that when the order to charge came—

"Another cry, terrible in its intensity and with foreboding wrath in its tones, filled the space. . . . From the throats of nearly six hundred Kentuckians rose the cry, 'Remember the Raisin!' They saw about them the forms of their murdered comrades and friends and relatives. They beheld the bedizened, painted savages, with barbarous cruelty, strike their wounded foes and casting their bodies, when dead or writhing, into the flames to be consumed. . . . It fell upon the ears of British regulars who themselves had been at the Raisin. In the fierce charge there was but one cry, oft repeated, but rising each time in sharper and sterner tones, 'Remember the Raisin, Remember the Raisin.' "

That day Tecumseh died, and Proctor lost his military reputation.

TRACKING THE BELL WITCH

The Bell Witch, called Kate by those who knew her, was one of the great phenomenons of Tennessee history. Perhaps the tale more properly belongs in the category of folklore.

In 1804 John Bell of North Carolina bought a thousand-acre tract of land in Robertson County on Red River. He then moved his large family to the spot near the village of Adams. The farm is about thirteen miles beyond Springfield and four miles from the Kentucky line.

The Bells were a large, prosperous, and happy farm family until about 1817, when the Bell Witch appeared.

"Kate" was a tergiversatorial witch—that is, she never appeared in human form. She was a weird and invisible apparition who came from "everywhere and nowhere," and her only object was to haunt and persecute the Bells.

John Bell, called "Old Jack" by the witch, was Kate's particular enemy, and she finally caused his death by poison.

Kate could sing, preach, quote scripture, engage in witticisms, and box the ears and tweak the noses of people who displeased her. She was a rough witch, and kindly disposed toward none but Mrs. John (Lucy) Bell. One of her favorite tricks was to snatch the covers off the beds as fast as they were made up.

In a more credulous age than this, people from all over the state were impressed by the doings of the Bell Witch. From miles around they converged on the lonely Bell farm to see and hear the strange goings-on. Kate never disappointed them.

After the death of John Bell in 1820, Kate departed "for seven

39

years," then she returned to haunt other members of the Bell family. A particular victim was Betsy Bell, who wanted to marry a young man named Joshua Gardner. Kate didn't approve, and the marriage never took place.

A half mile from the Bell farm there is a dense woods, with heavy undergrowth. Two small streams cross the road about two hundred yards apart.

All accounts have it that Andrew Jackson personally visited the Bells and had an encounter with the witch. Kate gave him a fine demonstration of her powers, putting a professional "witch layer" to flight, horse pistol, silver bullet, rabbit's foot, etc., notwithstanding.

En route to the house, between the two small streams, the witch stopped the wagon containing Jackson's camping equipment and provisions. The horses could not budge the wagon, even after the general greased the wheels, until the witch said, "You may go now, general. I'll see you later."

"By the eternal, boys," said the general, "this is worse than fighting the British!"

In 1828 the witch left again, this time to return in 107 years, which would have been 1935.

In 1934 Dr. Charles Bailey Bell of Nashville published a book about the Bell Witch, one of three which have been written on the ubiquitous ghost. He referred to the witch as a "spirit" and predicted her return "in another form" in 1935. Kate failed to show.

Two hundred yards from the old well and the site of the original Bell house, on the side of a hill, is the family burying ground where Kate's victim, John Bell, lies buried.

HISTORICAL LANDMARKS:
South of Nashville

Tusculum, which takes its name from the ancient villas around Rome, was very likely named by Judge John Haywood, a fairly early settler who lies buried on a hill beside the Cumberland Presbyterian Church.

Judge Haywood's home stood here at about the time of the Battle of New Orleans, in 1815. A giant of a man, learned in the law, he was the author of *Natural and Aboriginal History of Tennessee* and *Civil and Political History of Tennessee,* both published in 1823. These books gave the judge the title of "Father of Tennessee History," and he is still the most famous man who ever lived in Tusculum.

The site of the birthplace of John Bell is also near here. This distinguished Tennessean served in Congress and as secretary of war, and was once nominated for the presidency. He became, unfortunately, a political foe of Andrew Jackson, and thereafter was known by Tennessee Democrats as "The Great Apostate."

A highway marker for Dewitt Smith Jobe brings memories of a Confederate hero almost unknown in Civil War history. Like Sam Davis, he was a member of Coleman's Scouts. Captured in a cornfield in August, 1864, he swallowed the dispatches he was carrying. A patrol from the 15th Ohio Cavalry then mutilated and tortured Jobe to make him reveal the contents of the letters. He refused and was dragged to death behind a galloping horse.

41

At Chapel Hill a granite shaft surrounded by an iron fence marks the birthplace of Nathan Bedford Forrest, the Confederate "Wizard of the Saddle," generally considered to be the greatest cavalry commander on either side during the Civil War. Written on the marker is: "On this spot stood the pioneer cabin home of William and Miriam Beck Forrest. Here was born on the 13th day of July, 1821, their son, Nathan Bedford Forrest, lieutenant general, Confederate States of America and cavalry leader of world-wide fame, whose military tactics have become the standard of international armies."

Engraved on the tablet was a quotation from Forrest's farewell to his troops, delivered at Gainesville, Alabama, May 9, 1865: "I have never on the field of battle sent you where I was unwilling to go myself, nor would I now advise you to a course which I felt myself unwilling to pursue. You have been good soldiers, you can be good citizens. Obey the law. Preserve your honor."

This inscription, local residents say, is copied regularly by tourists who stop to admire the monument which was erected in 1927.

This old stone bridge near Fayetteville, which once spanned the Elk River, has now fallen into the stream.—Photo courtesy of the Tennessee Conservation Department.

The old stone bridge which spanned the Elk River near Fayetteville was hailed as an engineering marvel when it was completed in 1861, a few months before war struck Middle Tennessee. It consisted of six great spans or arches, was a hundred yards long, and cost $40,000—a considerable sum in 1861. The designers, however, made one grave error. One end of the bridge, which is on the main road to Huntsville, is lower than the other. As Killebrew stated it in *Resources of Tennessee*, it "has a declination of twelve degrees." This was just enough to prevent the driver of a wagon from seeing another wagon as it came upon the other end of the bridge.

Since there "was scarcely room to pass" on the bridge, one can suppose that many a farmer had harsh remarks to make as he tried to back up his mule team.

Specifications say the bridge is 315 feet long and fifteen feet wide, but that must be outside dimensions.

Sam Davis

SAM DAVIS AND DAVID CROCKETT

On the morning of November 27, 1863, young Sam Davis, a Confederate soldier in the service of Coleman's Scouts, stood on Seminary Hill at the edge of Pulaski. Perhaps the air was soft and sweet that morning, with blowing leaves and clouds foretelling rain. But when Sam Davis looked up, he saw a rope. The rope was a hangman's noose, and it was waiting for him.

Sam Davis didn't have to die. One word from him—the name of his commanding officer—and he could go free with a pass through the lines. But Sam Davis chose the rope. A witness wrote: "He died hard but brave."

It was not a suitable nor a merciful death for a soldier, struggling at the rope's end, face blackening in the choking strands. But that was the way Sam Davis chose to die, and because there are men who honor heroes, he has not been forgotten.

For ten years after the war the story of Sam Davis' death was almost unknown except to his family and a few friends. An account by J. B. Killebrew appeared in *Annals of the Army of Tennessee,* published in 1878 and later reprinted in *Military Annals of Tennessee.*

In the nineties S. A. Cunningham, editor of *The Confederate Veteran,* published in Nashville, became interested in the life and death of Sam Davis and determined to tell his story to the South and the nation. It has since been retold many times—one of the finest accounts of courage, devotion, and self-sacrifice to come out of the war.

Sam Davis was brought up on a farm in Rutherford County, on the banks of Stewart's Creek near Smyrna. The old farm

45

home, now owned by the state and operated by the Sam Davis
Memorial Association, stands near the field at Sewart Air Base,
and giant planes rise over the creek banks where Sam played
as a boy. When Sam was a youngster his father, Charles Louis
Davis, had 1,800 acres of land and scores of slaves, a comfortable
home, and a happy family. Sam was the youngest son.

As a boy, Sam enrolled as a student at the old Western
Military Institute, then a department of the University of Nashville. Montgomery Bell Academy at Nashville was also once
a department of the university, and students at MBA still sign
their names in the old book where Sam wrote his signature
more than a century ago.

Sam didn't stay in military school long, however. In April,
1861, he heard the bugles blow as civil war broke the nation
apart. In a matter of days he was in the Confederate army
as a member of the Rutherford Rifles of Murfreesboro, later
Company I of the First Tennessee Regiment of Volunteers under
Colonel George Maney. In the fall of that year he was in West
Virginia, fighting under Robert E. Lee and Stonewall Jackson.

When the Federal army invaded Tennessee and captured
Nashville, Sam Davis' outfit was ordered back to its home state.
Sam fought in the Battle of Shiloh in the spring of 1862, and
by his twenty-first birthday the next year he was a twice-
wounded veteran, now attached to Coleman's Scouts.

In November, 1863, Braxton Bragg's Confederate Army of
Tennessee was perched on the mountains around Chattanooga.
Within that city a Federal army under Generals Grant, Thomas,
and Sherman was busily engaged in bringing up reinforcements
from Corinth, Mississippi. A part of these reinforcements was
the Sixteenth Federal Army Corps under General Grenville M.
Dodge, which stopped at Pulaski, Tennessee, southwest of Columbia.

It was to investigate this troop movement that a number
of "scouts" (spies, the Federals called them) were sent to Middle
Tennessee, ostensibly under the command of "Captain E. Coleman."

These scouts, Sam Davis was one, were actually commanded
by Captain H. B. Shaw, who used the name Coleman to cover

his real identity. He also played the role of an itinerant doctor, moving freely behind Confederate and Federal lines.

It was the duty of Coleman's Scouts to gather information about the Federal forces that would be useful to Bragg's army. One member of the group, Joshua Brown, wrote an account of the capture and execution of Davis. Describing his own activities, Brown wrote: "I had counted almost every regiment and all the artillery in the Sixteenth Corps, and had found out they were moving on Chattanooga."

While on scout duty in Middle Tennessee Sam took advantage of the opportunity to visit briefly with his family in the farmhouse near Smyrna, hiding his horse behind a rock in the yard. On November 19, he rode south toward Alabama. When he reached Decatur he would start east on the so-called "scout line" toward Chattanooga.

As he neared the state line Sam was overtaken by two Federal scouts called jayhawkers, members of the Seventh Kansas Cavalry, men especially assigned to kill or capture Coleman's Scouts. One of the men, pretending to be a Confederate conscript officer, took Sam's pass, then disarmed him. And in Sam's boot and saddle seat were found various secret papers.

Sam was carrying maps of the Federal defenses around Nashville, and on the Nashville & Decatur Railroad, as well as detailed information on Federal troop movements. He had a letter from Coleman to General Bragg and toothbrushes and soap for the Confederate general.

How much of this information Sam had gathered himself, or how much had been given him by Coleman or others, we do not know. But General Dodge felt that there was a high-ranking traitor in Nashville or Pulaski who had given out the information, and he badly wanted his name. He had Sam brought to his headquarters.

"I told him he was a young man," General Dodge wrote, "and did not seem to realize the danger he was in.

" 'General Dodge,' said Sam, 'I know the danger of my situation, and I am willing to take the consequences!'

"I pleaded with and urged him with all the power I possessed

to give me some chance to save his life, for I had discovered
he was a most admirable young fellow. He then said:

"'It is useless to talk to me. I do not intend to do it . . .'"

Sam is also quoted as saying: "I know, General, that I shall
have to die, but I shall not tell where I got the information,
and there is no power on earth that can make me tell."

It seems likely that Sam was protecting his commanding
officer, Shaw, who was even then being held in the same jail,
unrecognized as Coleman, leader of the Scouts. Sam may or
may not have known the name of the Federal informant—the
secret Dodge wanted most. But certainly he felt that if he talked
he would betray his captain and his friends. As it was, Davis
died and Shaw was released.

In years after the war, General Dodge protested that he had
not wanted to hang Sam Davis, that Sam's obstinacy gave him
no other course. But the facts are these:

Sam was dressed in Confederate uniform, with the exception
of an old Federal overcoat which had been dyed brownish-black
by his mother to make it suitable for his use. This overcoat,
along with his boot, slit open by the Federals, and his canteen,
are on display at the Tennessee State Museum in Nashville.

A vital point was whether Sam was captured within Union
lines. Official records of his trial show that one witness said
he "considered" it within the lines, and another said, "I don't
know." Actually the lines were fluid at that time, and a reason-
able doubt existed.

Finally, it was not clear then and is not clear now whether
Sam Davis was a spy or simply a courier, carrying messages
to Bragg which had been given him by Coleman. This was the
gist of Sam's testimony at his trial—he had been given the papers
by Coleman for delivery to Bragg.

Sam had spoken bravely to General Dodge, but it must have
been hard for a boy of twenty-one, just entering manhood, to
face such a death. The night before his ordeal he wrote his
mother a pathetic letter, now preserved at the Davis home. It
reads:

"Dear Mother, Oh, how painful it is to write to you! I have
got to die tomorrow morning—to be hanged by the Federals.

Mother, do not grieve for me. I must bid you good-by forever-
more. Mother, I do not fear to die. Give my love to all. Your
Son, Sam Davis." In a postscript Sam wrote: "Mother, tell the
children all to be good. . . . Father, you can send after my remains
if you want to do so."

And so the morning of the 27th came. The drums rolled, and
Sam Davis, handcuffed, climbed on a wagon, sat on his coffin,
and rode to Seminary Hill. The night before, with Chaplain
James Young of the 81st Ohio Infantry, he had sung his favorite
song, "On Jordan's Stormy Banks I Stand."

At the scaffold Captain Armstrong, in charge of the execution,
was perhaps more shaken than Sam. "I would almost rather
die myself," he said. "I do not think hard of you," Sam replied.
"You are doing your duty."

Sam asked for news from the front, and was told Bragg's
army had lost the Battle of Missionary Ridge. He said, "I am
sorry to hear it, Captain. The boys will have to fight the battles
without me now."

When the last moment of life had come, Captain Chickasaw,
of Dodge's Scouts, rode up to the scaffold. He brought not a
reprieve, but a tempting offer. "Speak the name of your informant, and go home in safety."

Young Sam Davis shook his head. "No, I cannot. I had rather
die a thousand deaths than betray a friend, or be false to duty."

A Federal officer wrote long afterwards:
"The boy looked about him. Life was young and promising.
Overhead hung the noose; around him were soldiers in line;
at his feet was a box prepared for his body, now pulsing with
young and vigorous life; in front were the steps that would
lead him to disgraceful death, and that death was in his power
to so easily avoid. For just an instant he hesitated, and then
put aside forever the tempting offer. Thus ended a tragedy
wherein a smooth-faced boy, without counsel, in the midst of
enemies, with courage of highest type, deliberately chose death
to life secured by means he thought dishonorable."

John C. Kennedy, a neighbor of the Davises, went to Pulaski
for Sam's body, driving two mules hitched to a carryall. Sam's

younger brother, Oscar, went along on the grim, cold, and dangerous mission. They were able to get through, helped by sympathetic Yankees, and brought Sam's body home. It lies today in the quiet family cemetery, just back of the house.

Sam's home has been preserved as a shrine, and a bronze statue of him looks out over Nashville from Capitol Hill. At Pulaski another monument marks the place of his execution.

Poets have honored Sam. Ella Wheeler Wilcox wrote:

> Out of a grave in the Southland,
>   At the just God's call and beck,
> Shall one man rise with fearless eyes,
>   With a rope around his neck.

Farm boy, student, soldier in the ranks, Sam Davis taught a simple lesson that still lights a lamp for young men in darkness. He died because he chose to do his duty.

* * *

On the public square of Lawrenceburg is the statue of the man who "was born on a mountain in Tennessee," according to the popular song.

The statue was erected in 1922 in honor of the Tennessee bear hunter, Indian fighter, congressman, and hero of the Alamo. Beyond the town of Lawrenceburg, where Crockett was an early settler, is David Crockett State Park. The park contains Crockett Falls, on Shoal Creek, where David once owned a grist mill. A small museum features a modern version of the old grist mill.

It was in Lawrence County that Crockett's fortunes "began to take a rise," as he put it. He was elected a colonel of the militia, was sent to the state legislature at Murfreesboro and later to Congress. Crockett had moved there in 1817, the same year the county was organized.

Then he suffered a misfortune that resulted in his moving to West Tennessee. He wrote that the misfortune, "made a great change in my circumstances and kept me back very much in the world. I had built an extensive grist mill and powder mill,

David Crockett

all connected together, and also a distillery. They had cost me upwards of three thousand dollars, more than I was worth in the world.

"My mills were not blown up sky high, as you might guess, by my powder establishment, but swept away all to smash by a large fresh."

That determined restless David to pick up and pull out to West Tennessee. In later years he wrote books (or at least they appeared under his name) and became a political opponent of Andrew Jackson. He ended in Texas, dying gloriously as one of the defenders of the Alamo.

CUMBERLAND RIVER PEARLS

It was a good day for fishing back in 1881, or maybe it was 1882, when two Murfreesboro boys wet their lines in the Caney Fork River. Theirs was a strange catch.

The boys were Charles Bradford and James Johnson. At the mouth of Indian Creek they waded into the shallow stream and pulled up some mussels for bait. One of the boys opened a mussel shell and—so an old newspaper account says—a beautiful white pearl rolled out.

Old-time pearling men say it's not that easy—the pearl is always under the skin. But at any rate the boys had a pearl, a real "curiosity." They took it to Murfreesboro and turned it over to William Wendel, a druggist. He sent the pearl to Tiffany's in New York, and a few days later the boys had a check for $83. In those days that was quite a sum. Thus was started the colorful era of "pearling" on Middle Tennessee streams—an exciting time that lasted until World War I.

On the upper Cumberland and the Caney Fork, conditions were changed by the building of dams which slowed the current and covered bars with deep water. The mussels thrived in shoals and shallow places where fast-moving water brought them a constant food supply. In mud and sand they could "walk" on the bottom, moving slowly on a tough little "foot" which extended from the partly open shell.

With the deepening of the channels the little bivalves (they are of the genus *Unio*) lost their swift-running shoals. Many could no longer survive. In deep water they were less available to amateur pearlers who lacked special equipment, and conditions were apparently less favorable for producing pearls.

The building of the Great Falls Dam on the Caney Fork came along with the First World War, upsetting the living conditions of both mussels and people. Some pearls were found in the early twenties, but no fine pearls were reported after the war. This is partly due to the rising cost of labor. There are probably still some pearl-bearing mussels in the rivers, but there's too much labor involved to make it worthwhile looking for them.

In Stone's River there are mussels to be found—not until recent years has a dam been built on this tributary of the Cumberland. Albert Ganier, Sr., who owns a camp on the stream, has a large collection of shells but says he never found a pearl. Ganier thinks the pearl-armored mussels will disappear completely since the Percy Priest dam has been built.

What was it like in the old days, when pearlers by the hundreds armed themselves with broken case knives and waded into the streams? There are still some ex-pearlers around, and accounts in print tell of exciting times hunting the lustrous spheres.

In 1889 old-time pearler J. L. Smith moved to Nashville from Murfreesboro. He told a reporter for the *American* that the Caney Fork find had been the talk of the town in Murfreesboro, causing a mad rush to the creeks and rivers. The reporter wrote that thousands "nay millions of the quiet bivalves" were pulled up from their beds of mud and sand and split open in the search for pearls. Now and then a pearl appeared, and the hunt went on.

The branches of Stone's River below Murfreesboro had been "made barren" of mussels, Smith reported, though others appeared there in later years. Above Murfreesboro, he added, the pearls were worthless. Caney Fork, he said, was "about worked out," and the search was still going on.

Perhaps the most appealing account of a Tennessee pearl hunt ever written appeared in the *New Yorker* magazine of July 28, 1951. It was written by the Lebanon novelist Bowen Ingram. In it she told her experience as a child on the Caney Fork, where she pulled up mussels on a bar to make a longed-for necklace of seed pearls. Bowen (Mrs. Dan) Ingram has that necklace today—and there are other possessors of Caney Fork and Cumberland River pearls. Not all were sold—and perhaps dozens are being worn in rings and necklaces by Tennessee women today.

Mrs. Ingram's father, Austin Prewett, lived in Gordonsville, where he "dabbled" in pearls and farming in the placid years before World War I, splashing in his Marathon automobile across the shallow Caney Fork. He bought pearls and sold them to Black, Starr & Frost in New York—and kept some for his daughter. When his grandson, Dan Ingram, Jr., was married, his bride wore a ring set with three lustrous pearls from the Caney Fork.

One of the most famous mussel beds and pearling grounds was below Carthage on the Cumberland. Five miles below the town, near Taylor's Landing, was Roland's Towhead (island) and a big bar where mussels thrived. Here, so far as we know, was held the only "public pearling" in the history of Middle Tennessee. It was a fine Sunday with about fifty couples on hand. Everybody got excited when one swain, having found a small pearl, hid it in a mussel his sweetheart was opening. The girl almost fainted for joy when the pearl appeared.

Overton A. High, ninety, known to his friends as Obe, was an ambitious pearler on the upper Cumberland around Carthage in the days before Lock 7 covered the shallow places. High remembers when John Bowman and Al Napier found two-hundred dollars worth of pearls in less than a week, and Bowman bought a fifteen-acre "hill farm" with his share of the money. That was back in 1897. High listed the types of mussels found in those days as Heel Splitters or Bull Heads, Ladies' Pocket-books (good pearlers), and Pinks. He recalled a mussel bed above Rome about a mile long, where many tons of mussels were found.

Owners of pearl necklaces still follow some old advice—if you own pearls, wear them. Pearls contain a small amount of water, and if they are worn and allowed to show their luster, they look forever young. Pearls hidden in a vault, so it is said, will lose their life and lustrous beauty. It was not unusual for pearl buyers to peel a dull pearl like an onion, removing layers until

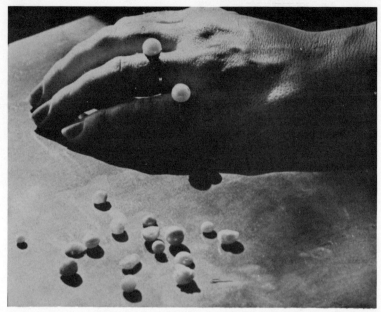

Shown are rings set with pearls from the Cumberland or Caney Fork and a scattering of unset baroque pearls.

the luster was restored. "I saw my father peel a big pearl," Sam Key, son of pearl buyer T. O. Key, of Carthage, said. "He sold it to a fellow who kept it in a glass of water, but the pearl died anyway." Carmack Key, Sam's brother, has a delicate scale which his father used to weigh the pearls.

Herman Myer of Carthage was called the "Pearl King," buying large numbers of pearls and selling them to Tiffany's. Myer moved to New York, where he continued in the pearl business and other enterprises until his death in 1944.

Mrs. Edward M. Turner of Carthage, related by marriage to the Myer family, wears Cumberland River pearls from the Myer collection. Her rings are set with lustrous white pearls as large as English peas.

"Rosebuds" or pink pearls are still noted for their beauty. A fine example is one owned and worn by Mrs. Stanley Horn,

Jr., of Brentwood, the granddaughter of Marvin Ford, a noted pearl buyer. Mrs. Horn remembers that her grandfather dealt in pearls at McMinnville and that he went to New York twice a year to sell them to Tiffany's. Ford once paid two thousand dollars for a river pearl—perhaps the highest price ever paid in Tennessee. He later sold it to Mrs. Nicholas Roosevelt Longworth, daughter of President Theodore Roosevelt.

Many a pearl buyer gave his children a tobacco sack full of "slugs" or misshapen pearls, some lustrous and iridescent. These were worthless in those days—but they may not be worthless now. Walter Sharp, former chairman of the Fine Arts Department at Vanderbilt University, reports that beautiful and valuable jewelry is now being made in Italy from gold worked around misshapen pearls—and in fact beautiful things have been made from these "baroque" or imperfect pearls since the days of Benvenuto Cellini, the great Italian artisan who used them himself.

"It is quite likely," said Sharp, "that developing tastes in this country may now encompass these formerly disregarded pearls—or 'slugs' as the old pearlers called them—and they will yet be of real value."

Mussels are still being taken in large quantities from the Tennessee River. And mussel boats equipped with "mules" (underwater sails) and "brails" (rakes) for bringing up the bivalves have been operating on the Cumberland just above Nashville.

Many tons of the shells are being shipped to Kobe, Japan, with some low-grade pearls being found in the process.

The Japanese make small pellets from these shells and insert them under the skins or "mantles" of live oysters, who then cover the pellets with layers of nacre. In due time the oyster is opened and a lustrous "cultured" pearl is removed—a pearl born from a Tennessee mussel shell. The chances are good that it will be sold in the United States.

The Japanese also make pearl buttons from mussel shells, although modern plastics have hurt this business. One pearl button factory still operating in this area is Weber & Sons Button Co. at Savannah, a Tennessee River town where hundreds of driveways are paved with broken mussel shells.

Mussel diggers on the Tennessee still find some pearls when cooking the meat from the shells. Most of these are low-grade slugs which bring about six dollars an ounce, but once in a while a biscuit-shaped pearl worth twenty-five to fifty dollars will turn up.

The disappearance of fine pearls from the Tennessee is probably due more to the great amount of digging than to current or stream changes. So many mussels are taken that they don't have time to produce good pearls. The present mussel harvest produces smaller, younger pearls.

Prehistoric Indians of Middle Tennessee ate millions of mussels, and shells are found in heaps around their townsites. The meat of Tennessee varieties is tough, and never referred to as the "succulent bivalve."

The shallow waters and bars are almost gone now, and perhaps never again will lustrous pearls be taken from Tennessee mussels, but the fortunate owners of these beauties have souvenirs of exciting treasure hunts on Tennessee rivers.

BLACK FOX

Black Fox was the only warlike chief who ever lived in Middle Tennessee, and he only camped here in the winter season.

Early historians called Black Fox a friendly (?) Indian, and the question mark is theirs. The settlers bought venison and skins from the Fox, but they didn't trust him.

The hunting home of Black Fox, Fox Camp Spring, is in Rutherford County just outside Murfreesboro. In the late summer of 1792 Abraham Castleman, finest scout in the Cumberland country, silently studied the ground around the big spring and found what he was looking for—the tracks and signs of hundreds of hostile Indians.

Putnam's *History of Middle Tennessee* says of Abe Castleman: "He was fearless, with a quick sight and a sure shot. He made no noise or tramp as he walked and with his body a little bent, he seemed ever looking for Indians or marks on trees."

Black Fox was gone, though the hunting season was not yet over. It all spelled trouble to Castleman, and he reported what he had seen to Fort Nashboro. At first the settlers were alarmed, then relieved, then sarcastic as nothing happened. Castleman, they said, had "smelled at a cold trail."

As for the scout, he quietly remarked that he was "going over to Buchanan's to see the enemy." He did, and the enemy struck the fort that night, hundreds strong. The Indians were driven off after their famous chief, Shawnee Warrior, was killed and another chief, John Watts, wounded.

Whether Black Fox joined the raiders or simply "made himself scarce" was never known, but he lived on the Hiwassee River for many years, and later signed two treaties with the white men. By the terms of one of these, a treaty of cession of lands, the Fox, called Enolee by his own people, received a guarantee of a hundred dollars a year for the rest of his life. In 1810 the old chief signed another treaty by which he agreed to give up forever the old tribal law of blood vengeance and live in peace.

Also near Murfreesboro is the great limestone rock which marks the geographical center of the state, but like Fox Camp Spring it is outside the town and seldom seen. Another of Murfreesboro's tourist attractions is Oaklands, the old Maney home at the north end of Maney Street. Oaklands has been beautifully restored, furnished as it was in plantation days, and opened to the public as a museum house. Built in stages, the mansion was a great social center in prewar days when cotton was king. It was in this house that General Nathan B. Forrest received the surrender of a Federal force during the Civil War.

CHATTANOOGA

From the days when true sports wore heavy gold watch chains and detachable collars and cuffs, Chattanooga has been a favorite honeymoon retreat. Tall, stone-faced mountains, wooded ridges, a fertile plain, and a winding, shining river weave Chattanooga's spell on young lovers, not-so-young married folks, and plain everyday tourists.

Chattanooga lies in the narrow gap of the Cumberland Mountains through which passes the Tennessee River. Approaching Moccasin Bend one can see Raccoon Mountain, and great Walden's Ridge, with Signal Mountain as its southernmost tip, stretches away toward the northeast. The ridge honors the memory of Elisha Walden, a long hunter who came into the country in the 1760s.

The sheer face of Lookout Mountain reaches toward the sky, rising 2,250 feet above sea level and 1,700 feet above low watermark of the Tennessee.

Below the twisting bend of the river lies Chattanooga, nestled between the Tennessee and wooded, rocky Missionary Ridge. The ridge, five hundred feet high, runs north and south from Trueblood Hill to the vicinity of Rossville. Pierced by two highway tunnels, it separates downtown Chattanooga from a fast-growing suburban district out Brainerd road.

As a modern city, Chattanooga had its beginning about 1815, when the Scotch-Cherokee chief John Ross established a landing, warehouse, and ferry about a mile from the start of the great bend which forms the Moccasin. To the south of Ross'

61

Chattanooga as seen from atop Lookout Mountain. Photo courtesy the Tennessee Conservation Department.

store in a gap of the mountains just over the Georgia line was Rossville.

Chattanooga received its present name and was laid out as a town after the removal of the Cherokees in 1838. A start was made the previous year. According to Miss Zella Armstrong, historian of the Chattanooga *Times,* the name is Creek in origin, the "Creek Path" passing near the city. The original word was "Chat-to-to-noo-gee" meaning "rock coming to a point or overhanging bluff."

In the early years after the Civil War, Chattanooga, with large coal and iron deposits in the mountains around the city, had visions of becoming the iron smelting and blast furnace center of the South. With the aid of outside capital, mostly English, a promising start was made.

After a frantic period of boom and bust, featured by wild land speculation, the bubble burst. Because of thin veins and the high phosphorous content of the ore, the blast furnaces could not make acceptable steel. Birmingham, not Chattanooga, became the Vulcan of Dixie.

However, the energetic citizens had other strings to their bow, and today Chattanooga has more than 440 industrial plants producing over fifteen-hundred different articles. The University of Chattanooga, the Cadek Conservatory of Music, and the Baylor and McCallie schools for boys are located in the city.

Chattanooga's attractions are so many and varied that it is well to spend a night or two at one of the many hotels or tourist courts and take at least two days to see them all.

Lookout Mountain Incline Railway is one of the steepest and most scenic incline railways in the world. It is forty-five hundred feet long with an elevation of fourteen-hundred feet and a grade of nearly one foot in three at the steepest place. Its two cars, pulled by steel cables straight up the sides of the mountain, are equipped with numerous safety devices. Known as "Incline No. 2" (another such railway had been built previously) it began operation in November of 1895 and has operated continuously since.

Point Park near the incline terminal on Lookout Mountain, is a federal battlefield marking a part of the Battle of Chattanooga, or Missionary Ridge, fought November 23-25, 1863. From the terrace of the Adolph Ochs observatory and museum, one can see the city of Chattanooga, Moccasin Bend, and the entire maneuver area of the two armies during the battle. For generations writers have wheeled up their heaviest adjectives to describe the overwhelming view from the point and from Sunset Rock, another knuckle on the finger of the mountain.

Cameron Hill is a high point on West Sixth Street, on the east side of the river. It offers a wonderful view of the countryside.

Chickamauga Battlefield is a part of the same federal reservation that includes Point Park, Missionary Ridge, and Orchard Hill. Here in September 1863, the Federal army of the Cumberland, under General W. S. Rosecrans, was defeated by the Confederate army of Tennessee, under General Braxton Bragg.

On the highway approaching Chattanooga are scores of signs on barns and birdhouses advising everyone to "See Rock City." This great attraction is the work of both man and nature. Rock City offers all the beauty of a wild, craggy mountain, with great

weathered rocks thrust against the sky, and a doll-like city
peeping through the haze below.

One of the "extras" at Rock City is the famous "camera
obscura" which, on a giant screen, presents a panorama of the
scenery around the mountain as the viewers stand inside the
lens. It is in the man-made Fairyland Caverns that children
get their biggest thrills. Rocks of beautiful quartz and other
minerals from around the country mark the entrance, and inside
are stalagtites and rock formations from various caves in the
mountain. But what delights children most are the dwarfs,
gnomes, elves, and fairies, living in their own villages and houses
just as in the storybooks.

Not far from Monteagle is Sewanee, the beautiful "domain"
of the University of the South.

Sewanee, as the school is generally called, is a liberal arts
college with an enrollment of 830. Founded before the Civil War
by the Episcopal Church it stresses "depth rather than scatter,"
with "wide exposure to the full-range of human thought."

Sewanee's buildings are constructed of native sandstone, similar to that used in Christ Church Episcopal in Nashville. The
predominant theme is Gothic, with cottages in the English
tradition.

Centerpiece of those beautiful buildings is All Saints' Chapel,
dedicated to the benefactors of Sewanee. Used by the students
for daily services, the chapel contains a mighty organ of seventy
ranks, numbering between three and four thousand pipes.

The Polk carillon in Shapard Tower has fifty-six bells, and
is one of the world's largest. The nearby Breslin Clock Tower
is one of the oldest on the campus.

THE FORT BLOUNT TRAIL

In 1787, wrote historian John Haywood, the North Carolina legislature authorized militia officers of Davidson and Sumner counties to appoint two or more persons to mark out a road from the lower end of Clinch Mountain to the Cumberland Settlement.

"Soon afterward," says Judge Haywood, "a road was cut from Bledsoe's Lick (Castalian Springs) into the Nashville Road leading to Clinch River."

This was the Fort Blount Road early travelers took from North Carolina to Nashville, and their accounts never ceased to rail against its mud, mountains, rocks, and general cussedness. It is still no boulevard and only partly paved, but it has no real impediments to automobiles.

The best way to get on the Fort Blount Road is to drive to Gallatin and swing east on Highway 25 to Castalian Springs and Hartsville. If this is not exactly on the old road bed, it is at least within a few hundred yards of it.

At Payne's Store the east-west and north-south routes intersect. Here, or very near here, stood the village of Green Garden, listed by the *Gazeteer* in 1834 as a "post office" three miles east of Castalian Springs. The village and even the name are lost to memory.

On the outskirts of Hartsville is Goose Creek and the beautiful bluegrass valley which was once the plantation of Colonel Tilman Dixon, one of the earliest settlers on the road. Many early travelers, including Prince Louis Phillipe of France, stopped at the Dixon house, which served as a tavern in pioneer days. Built

about 1788, the house has two brick wings which were added
before the Civil War. Still standing near the big spring where
it was built, the house has been restored and opened to the
public as a museum house.

During the 1790s the Fort Blount Road running east from
Dixon Springs had to compete with the Caney Fork Road, which
ran south to William Walton's ferry at the junction of the
Cumberland and the Caney Fork.

About five miles from Dixon Springs, just beyond Defeated
Creek at Difficult, is the old spring where the stream got its
name. According to Haywood, it happened this way:

On March 2, 1786, John Peyton, a surveyor, Ephriam Peyton,
Thomas Pugh, and John Frazier made camp for the night at
this spring. At midnight, as the men slept soundly, Indians took
advantage of the soft snow to surround the camp and open
fire, wounding three of the sleepers. All the men were able to
make their way separately to the Cumberland settlement, leaving their horses and property in the hands of the Indians.

Years later Peyton wrote to the Cherokee chief responsible
for this incident and requested the return of his compass, a
valuable brass instrument used in surveying.

"As for you, John Peyton," the chief replied, "I have taken
your 'land stealer' and broken it against a tree."

About five miles from Difficult is the community of Gladdice,
just below Bagdad. The original "Fort Blount Branch Road"
passed through Bagdad and followed Salt Lick Creek, which
runs toward the Cumberland on the left side of the road.

Fort Blount Road goes to Williamsburg, named for Captain
Sampson Williams, who came to the Cumberland country with
James Robertson in 1779. Williams moved to Fort Blount after
serving two terms as sheriff of Davidson County. In 1799 he
was representing Sumner County in the state senate and was
living at Fort Blount, later Williamsburg, at the time. He later
became Smith County court clerk.

Jackson County's first jail, a tiny building of stout logs, still
stands near the home of Rupert Jones north of the river. The
"saddle and rider" construction of this log cabin was very se-
curely mortised and joined. A tumble-down little building

nearby was the office of the first sheriff of Jackson County, and his iron gun racks are still fastened to the wall.

There is historical controversy of long standing as to whether Fort Blount stood north or south of the river, but modern historians have concluded that the fort was on the north side of the general course of the river—actually west of the stream as it curves north and south.

Williamsburg was north of the river, and it was here that Sampson Williams, first commander at Fort Blount, lived and died. The fort was built in 1792 and named for Territorial Governor William Blount in 1794. It was abandoned as a military post in 1796.

Early travelers reported that Williams converted the old fort into a "large house," and one traveler wrote that Fort Blount was "about to be rebuilt." Since it was never rebuilt as a military post, this apparently refers to the conversion of the fort to a private home.

The location of Williamsburg is known beyond a doubt because that sturdy little log jail has defied time and weather to this day. A number of log houses still standing in the vicinity offer evidence of the antiquity of the settlement. Historian Alvin Wirt wrote that the county seat was moved from Williamsburg to Gainesboro in 1817, "and the place was thereafter called Fort Blount."

Smith County was formed from a part of Sumner in 1799 and two years later Jackson County was formed, including Fort Blount. It is likely the jail was built at that time.

HAPPY CLANG OF THE DINNER BELL

It was in 1830, during the administration of President Andrew Jackson, that long hunter Edmund Jennings found deer and other animals drinking from a certain spot in the creek. He marked the spot with "bee gum" and a length of cane; when he returned to civilization, he spread the news of the salt lick with the cold water spring in the middle of the creek.

In 1840 a new settler named Shepherd Kirby found that the spring water cured his ailing eyes, and for more than a century now summertime visitors have congregated on Red Boiling Springs to "take the waters" for sake of health and well-being. There have been hundreds of testimonials on the wonderful healing powers of the waters.

Most of the "mineral springs" that were so popular in Tennessee a half-century ago are gone now and all but forgotten. For example, Macon County's Epperson Springs, which competed with Red Boiling Springs back in 1880, is no longer mentioned.

Red Boiling, however, has defied the trend and is today a thriving resort with three hotels operating during the summer months to serve guests from all parts of the country.

The Cloyd, a modern brick hotel on the Gainsboro road, boasts fifty-six rooms, private baths, a bowling alley, bathhouse, and swimming pool. It is operated by Mrs. Dora King and owned by Dr. A. T. Hall of Lebanon.

The Donoho, next door, boasts the longest colonnaded porch in town. It also has been recently remodeled with new beds and private bathrooms and is famous for its home-cooked meals. It is owned and operated by Mr. and Mrs. Edgar Hagan.

Red Boiling's famous old Palace Hotel is gone now, and in its place stands a modern rest home. Guests at the Palace a few years ago will remember its magnificent facade of porches and columns—longer than a football field. Its lobby, furnished entirely in wicker furniture, was reminiscent of the "resort days" of the nineties.

The Counts, a year-around hotel, is operated by Mr. and Mrs. Hobart Clark.

Red Boiling has other attractions which equal or surpass its famous waters. At an elevation of fourteen hundred feet above sea level, it is nearly a thousand feet higher than Nashville. The sun can get hot, but humidity is less, and air conditioners aren't really necessary.

The valley of Salt Creek lies in a dimple of the Highland Rim, with the white-columned hotels rising between long lines of hills. The valley was nameless, and on our first visit there we described it as "Veranda Valley."

Guests arriving at this rural haven can "take out"—to borrow an expression from the late Governor Henry Horton—and forget the cares and problems of city life. At Red Boiling Springs there is little to worry about and not much to do. The town has one industry, a garment plant, but still no whistles blow.

The most familiar—and happiest—sounds are the crowing roosters and cooing doves. But the sweetest sound of all is the happy clang of the brass dinner bell, calling hungry guests to tables piled high with country ham, fried chicken, green beans, and all the old-fashioned fixings.

With square dances on Saturday night and preaching on Sunday morning, there's lots of time left for swimming, shooting the breeze, and exercising the rocking chairs. Veranda Valley is truly a place to put your feet up, and catch up on rest.

BIG WATER IN THE HILLS

The Upper Cumberland country is just as pretty as folks from up there say it is, and that's going some.

Clay County was created in 1870 by the Tennessee Constitutional Convention. Celina, Butler's Landing, and Bennett's Ferry contested for the honor of being the county seat—Celina won the election. At that time the town had only three hundred inhabitants.

Celina was named for Celina Fisk, widow of Moses Fisk, the first clerk of the Smith County Court and one of the most famous and best educated of the pioneers in the Upper Cumberland Country. Another account has it that the town was named by a family which had just moved there from Celina, Ohio.

Celina Fisk owned much of the land on which Celina was built. Her husband had been a pioneer road builder and founder of the village of Hilham in Overton County. He, along with Sampson Williams, founded the Fisk Female Academy, one of the first schools for girls in the state.

Dale Hollow, named for the Dale family, is on the Obey River, a winding mountain stream which meanders from east to west. It receives the waters of the Wolf River and in turn empties into the Cumberland near Celina.

The dam is three miles east of Celina. Operated by the U.S. Army Corps of Engineers, it has four generators which could supply the electrical needs of a city of 45,000 people. The great dam, two hundred feet high and nearly two thousand feet long, also serves to control floods on the Obey and Cumberland. It

71

contributes to the navigability of the Cumberland during low water.

Here indeed is big water in the hills—the tiny channel of the Obey now a broad expanse of clear water, reaching up the valleys, the coves, and the fingers as it threads its way through the highlands.

Near the Celina end of the lake is Dale Hollow Creek, Horse Creek Cove, Indian Creek, and Kyle Branch, all favorite haunts of fishermen. The more adventurous rod and reelers go many miles eastward up the lake to fish the coves and creeks.

Dale Hollow Lake—an expanse of blue water with wooded shores.—Photo courtesy Tennessee Conservation Department.

Inside the library at Rugby—story on page 23.—Photo by Louis C. Williams.

The tragedy at Frenchtown—story on page 27.—Painting by Jim Young.

*Lover's Leap in Rock City Gardens—story on page 61.—Photo
courtesy Tennessee Conservation Department.*

*The covered bridge on the Red—story on page 72.—Photo
by Louis C. Williams.*

Fall Creek Falls—story on page 87.—Photo courtesy Tennessee Conservation Department.

Torch throwing in Mammoth Cave—story on page 109.

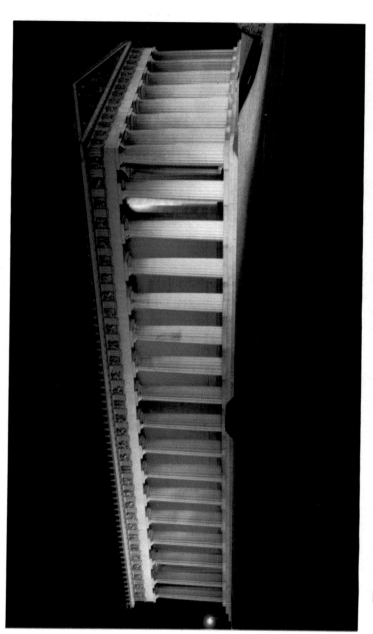

The Parthenon—story on page 143.—Photo courtesy Tennessee Conservation Department.

Reelfoot Lake—story on page 219.—Photo courtesy Tennessee Conservation Department.

PORT ROYAL ON THE RED

On an April morning in 1780 Moses Renfroe, poling his boat up the Cumberland with John Donelson and his fleet, came to the mouth of Red River.

Renfroe liked the looks of the little stream and the red soil on its banks. His boat fell out of line and moved slowly up the Red. The Donelson flotilla continued up the Cumberland to the French Lick settlement that would one day be the capital of Tennessee.

Today, a mile below the great river town of Clarksville, the Red flows into the Cumberland from the east as quietly as it did in 1780. No boats, except for an occasional fishing boat, move between its banks. Fallen trees, stumps, and snags choke its channel.

Gar fish, looking lean and lazy, float just below the surface. Industrial wastes from plants near Clarksville pollute the water.

The Red was not always such a silent stream. A century ago the voices of flatboat men, hauling tobacco from Port Royal, echoed off its banks, and before the turn of the century the deep whoom of steamboat whistles made farm boys come running.

That was in the old days, when Port Royal competed with Nashville and Murfreesboro to become the capital of Tennessee, and its citizens saw themselves at a crossroads, and at the junction of the Red and the Sulphur Fork, strategically located to become a thriving metropolis.

Port Royal, twelve miles east of Clarksville by road and fifty miles on the meandering little river, was founded in 1797 on a thirty-acre tract owned by Samuel Wilcox. He was a native of Port Royal, South Carolina, and must have given the village its name.

In 1834 the *Tennessee Gazeteer* said that "a number of flatboats are annually built at Port Royal for the shipment of tobacco." At Clarksville the cargoes could move to the Ohio, the Mississippi, and New Orleans—a great trip for an inland farm boy who wanted to see the world.

In 1876 the *Gazeteer* listed four business houses in the ambitious village on the Red—W. M. Bourne Grocery and the general stores of Darden & Weatherford, Halliburton & Son, and B. R. Miller.

In the early years Port Royal dueled with Clarksville over the status of the Red—was it or was it not a navigable stream? Port Royal shippers wanted it open for navigation, while Clarksville residents wanted to build dams between its high banks and pen up its power for water-driven mills. The battle shifted back and forth, but Clarksville prospered and Port Royal did not. Even so, the flatboats still moved downstream, and Killebrew reported in 1874 that "chickens and turkeys, in great droves, were compelled to take compulsory voyages of a thousand miles."

In the 1830s the "silkworm fever" hit Port Royal and Clarksville. Mulberry trees were planted and silkworms hatched, but the plan came to grief. A man sent to England to buy silk reeling machinery absconded with the money.

In the eighties there was still enough business up the Red to justify a weekly trip to Port Royal by the *Julien Gracey,* a ramshackle little steamer called a "top water boat" by river men. This little packet, built in Clarksville in 1880, called regularly at Port Royal, Mouth of Harpeth, and Dover.

Today, where the *Julien Gracey* once plied her trade, the Red River is filled with mud, waste materials, snags, and fallen trees. The river is navigable for less than five miles from its mouth.

Once, in the long ago, the U.S. Government put up five thousand dollars to clean out the Red, and certainly the river needs it today. It seems a shame that this beautiful, natural stream

*Trees and snags mark the head of navigation on
Red River, about three miles from its mouth.*

should be choked and clogged because of indifference and ne-
glect.

The valley of the Red, between Clarksville and Port Royal,
is a rich, colorful valley with the dark green leaves of the world-
famous "Clarksville" tobacco standing out against the red soil.
Whiteface and Angus cattle dot the fields, some standing belly
deep in ponds to beat the heat.

Little remains of the once prosperous river town that aspired
to be capital of Tennessee. The little covered bridge built in
1903 still stands but is in need of restoration. A great brick
storehouse, once a Masonic hall, is abandoned to bats and
pigeons. There is not a going business left in Port Royal. The
Red is cleaner here, fifty miles upstream, and the croaking of
bullfrogs is the only sound to be heard in the village.

The old "Chinese Temple" post office in Clarksville.

THE CUMBERLAND TO CLARKSVILLE

The Cumberland, once the Chauvanon or Shawanoe (river of the Shawnees) was first mentioned in historical records by the French explorer Marquette in 1675, seven years before any historian mentioned the Tennessee.

At French Lick (Nashville) on the Cumberland lived the French-Shawnee Peter Chartier, and his father before him, the first white men who came to Middle Tennessee. They lived and traded with the Shawnees.

Ramsey's *Annals* tells how the harassed Shawnees, the "Gypsies of the Forest," determined to abandon Nashville by water. But the Chickasaws were waiting for them "above the mouth of the Harpeth," where the island narrows the course of the river, and every Shawnee was slain in the ambush. Ramsey dates this ancient river battle about 1715.

In the early days of the Middle Tennessee settlements, before the coming of railroads and highways, the Cumberland was a great trade route. Before the Civil War, regular steamboat runs took cotton, tobacco, molasses, and other items to New Orleans via the Ohio and the Mississippi, while hardware and fancy manufactured goods came to Nashville merchants from New York and Pennsylvania. Once iron bars from the furnaces of Montgomery Bell and other "iron masters" on the Harpeth River and Sycamore Creek went down the Cumberland.

Vanus Neely, with the U.S. Corps of Engineers, says river traffic on the Lower Cumberland is heavier than ever before, and tonnages of gasoline, sand, gravel, steel, and scrap moved to and from Nashville are greater than they ever were in the old days. Above Nashville, however, there is now very little commercial traffic on the river. However, the Engineers are now more aware and more concerned than ever before with the welfare and needs of boaters, outboard and inboard, who travel on the river and ride on the lakes for fun.

One of the biggest problems on Cheatham Reservoir at Nashville is pollution of the stream by wastes from industrial plants on the waterfront.

Eight miles down the river is Lock B, and fifteen miles beyond is the mouth of historic Red River where the Civil War earthworks of Fort Providence still mark the bluff.

It was here, at the mouth of the Red, that Moses Renfroe went ashore from Donelson's flotilla in the spring of 1780 and built a cabin for his family. Here too, in pioneer days, shipments of tobacco and other produce from the old town of Port Royal came from Red River into the Cumberland, to float down to New Orleans.

The first survey of the Cumberland was made in 1768 by young Lieutenant Thomas Hutchins, the first and only civil "Geographer of the United States." He drew the first map of the Cumberland showing the Red, the Harpeth (he called it the Fish) and Stone's Rivers. Historian S. C. Williams says, "This is the first map showing the environs of Clarksville and Nashville." It is still in existence, owned by the Pennsylvania Historical Society.

The building occupied by the Clarksville Light & Power Company resembles an oriental temple. Manager Jesse F. Perry told the story of the building, which was once a post office.

Before the turn of the century a young American architect had been captured and held prisoner by unfriendly Chinese. All he could see from his prison window was a Chinese temple. He came home later to practice his trade, and in 1898 was commissioned to build a post office in Clarksville. He built a replica of the temple he had seen from his jail window—but instead of dragons he put four American eagles at the corners.

THE CANEY FORK

Here's a river that's still a river, as wild and rugged as it ever was, with two shining lakes to boot! Green cane grew head high in Middle Tennessee's lowlands 150 years ago, sheltering Indians and animals from the rifles of the white men. From these forests of waving cane, the little river got its name.

McMinnville is in Caney Fork country. The great spurs of the Cumberland Mountains extend across the eastern horizon, from north to south, and the Collins and the Barren Fork, two of the Caney Fork's lusty tributaries, make a junction just below the town.

McMinnville, one of the most beautiful Middle Tennessee towns, stands on an elevated peninsula (a thousand feet above sea level) formed by the Barren Fork, and the surrounding mountains rise another thousand feet.

The great mountain to the south is called Ben Lomond, a name suggestive of Scotland's glens. Five miles to the east are the twin peaks of the Cardwell Mountains. Around to the north-west boldly rises the great bulk of Short Mountain, where the waters of little Mountain Creek turned the power wheels of early textile factories in the years before the Civil War.

Of all the dams in the Tennessee and Cumberland valleys, Great Falls is perhaps the most unique. Here man has changed the face of nature to serve his ends—yet the rugged look of the land has lost none of its charm. The Caney Fork "takes its rise," says Killebrew's *Resources of Tennessee,* "in the Cumberland tableland, about eighteen miles east of Sparta. Running southward, and then west, it descends through a deep, narrow

79

gorge, hemmed in by beetling cliffs, and characterized by wild
scenery. Emerging into the valley, it passes westward, by many
devious windings among the romantic hills to the Big Falls below
Rock Island, where it plunges down into a long, winding, and
narrow valley leading out into the Great Central Basin of Middle
Tennessee."

The historians of seventy-five years ago could not foresee the
engineering feat that was to come during the First World War,
when engineers of the old Tennessee Electric Power Company
harnessed the waters of the Caney Fork. "The railroad crossed
on a bridge half a mile above the falls, near Rock Island," wrote
Killebrew, "and from this point the impetuous river plunges
down one fall after another, descending ninety-four feet within
two miles." Here, just below the junction of the Caney Fork,
the Collins, and the Rocky River, the engineers built their dam,

The Caney Fork River.—Photo courtesy
Tennessee Conservation Department.

forcing the water back into the Collins, drying up the Caney Fork for three quarters of a mile where the falls were steepest.

At the point where the swollen Collins passed near the dry bed of the Caney Fork a tunnel was dug and water turned through the penstocks of a powerhouse below. To this day the water, falling 150 feet, turns the turbines of two generators to produce a maximum of 35,000 kilowatts of electricity per hour—enough to supply a fair-sized town.

Across Snow's Hill and past Cove Hollow Dock is Center Hill Dam—the latest and biggest impoundment on the Caney Fork. This great dam, built by the Army Corps of Engineers in 1949 and still operated by the Engineers, is 250 feet high and 2,160 feet long. Its three generators are rated at 135,000 kilowatts.

The hill-circled lake at Center Hill is a fisherman's paradise. It has seven large commercial docks, some offering restaurant and cabin facilities. Many sportsmen own fishing camps and boathouses in the green hollows and coves for which the lake is famous. Below the dam the Caney Fork resumes its identity as a winding river.

A road runs along the river bank to Lancaster and Carthage Junction. On the outskirts of Gordonsville the Trousdale Ferry Bridge crosses the Caney Fork to the old and historic road that led from Nashville to Knoxville. This little bridge, which creaks and groans at the mere sight of an approaching vehicle, makes a ninety-degree turn on its eastern approach, and the road leads to the ancient little town of Stonewall at the foot of Chestnut Mountain.

A mile and a half above Carthage the Benton McMillin Bridge crosses the Caney Fork, and a few hundred yards down the road the little river, far from its mountain source, makes a last graceful meander around Boulton's Bend and glides quietly into the Cumberland.

The Assembly Inn in Monteagle. It has burned
since this photograph was taken in 1957.

The colonnade porch
of the Beersheba
Springs hotel.
It overlooks the
Collins River Valley.

MONTEAGLE AND
BEERSHEBA SPRINGS

Monteagle

Monteagle, a two-street town on the mountain, is split squarely by a branch railroad running from Cowan to the coal mining town of Palmer. A sign on a water tank points out the Monteagle Sunday School Assembly. With winding roads, rustic bridges, and pleasant cottages, the Sunday School Assembly is a village within a village—a secluded mountaintop vacation spot that has drawn summer visitors for generations. An auditorium, clubhouse, theater, and 140 cottages comprise the community, which boasts its own water supply, sewerage system, and swimming pool.

The Assembly, organized in 1882, is made up of cottage owners from many states, about a third of them from Nashville and Middle Tennessee. Cottages are usually occupied only during the summer months with an eight-week season extending from July 1 to Labor Day. Visitors pay a small fee on entering the grounds, and cottages or rooms are sometimes available on a rental basis.

The Assembly was organized against a strong background of church and cultural influences, and the summer program reflects both these interests. There are prayer and church services, lectures, concerts, and movies almost every night during the season, besides many parties in the clubhouse and cottages. A daily program of planned activities includes swimming, hiking, games, and a kindergarten.

83

Beersheba Springs

For years there have been stories about this historic summer resort, and the first sight of that ancient and stately hotel, perched high on the brow of the mountain, is truly an exciting moment. From an elevation of about six hundred feet the colonnaded double gallery along the front of the hotel looks down on the green valley of the Collins River. Summer cottages, some of them built more than a century ago, share this view of the rolling countryside.

The hotel, now operated by the Assembly of the Methodist Church, has a long and colorful history. It is a coincidence that a great part of this beautiful resort was built by a philanthropic slave trader in the years just before the Civil War.

The history of Beersheba Springs begins in 1833, when Andrew Jackson was President. Mrs. Beersheba Porter Cain, wife of a prominent McMinnville businessman, discovered the fine "chalybeate" or mineral spring on top of the mountain, which made the resort possible and gave the site her name.

It was not until slave trader John Armfield bought the place in the early 1850s that Beersheba became famous as a resort. Armfield built the sixty-five-room hotel about 1852 although the dining room and the ballroom above it had been built well before that date. The wooden pegs which hold the structure together are as sound as the day they were driven into place.

Armfield built the "cross row" of cottages around the court in the rear of the hotel, some log and some brick, and many of them have resisted the wear and tear of time to this day. As his own home he built, on the bluff, the beautiful cottage now owned by Mrs. McPheeters Glasgow of Nashville.

Armfield never left Beersheba, although he eventually sold the hotel, and after the war he had a part in restoring the ravaged property. He died in 1871 and lies buried in a plot near his cottage.

In its palmiest days Beersheba was looked upon by Southern planters as a haven from the frequent scourges of yellow fever, typhoid, and cholera epidemics. In those days, and in these days, too, Middle Tennesseans were frequent visitors. Miss Louisa Thompson of McMinnville, who visited Beersheba long ago as a little girl, wrote:

"Late each afternoon large bonfires of pine knots were burned in front of the cabins, their brilliant flames not only frightening away wild animals and snakes—then a menace on the mountain—but giving light and warmth to the rooms."

Beersheba Springs is rich with stories and memories—glittering dances in the big ballroom, dark doings by bushwhackers in the Civil War, boyhood feats of skill and daring in the natural swimming pool of the Collins River.

CAVE AND WATERFALL

A tall mountain—a green valley—a deep cave—a high water-fall—a blue lake set in the hills—these are nature's masterpieces, and they are all included on a one-day trip south through Murfreesboro, Woodbury, and McMinnville, crossing Cumberland Mountain and swinging back to Nashville past Smithville and Center Hill Lake.

Early textile factories, run by water power, once stood along the road south of Woodbury, and according to a marker a grindstone factory was established on Short Mountain as early as 1806. It was on this road that the Cherokees passed on their historic "trail of tears" soon after Jackson's administration, on their way to a western reservation. Several Cherokees are buried along the road.

About four and a half miles from Woodbury on Cavendar Branch Road is Henpeck Mill. This overshot grist mill was built by William Neely in 1834 and operated until 1950.

Henpeck Mill got its name, so the story goes, from local wags who allowed that the mill ground so slowly that a dozen hens could eat the corn faster than the stones could grind it. A covered chute, or conveyor for the water from a powerful spring in the hillside, led down to the mill and provided its power—an almost incredible looking arrangement in this day of gasoline and electricity.

South of Woodbury is Warren County, famed for its sorghum molasses, and McMinnville, the county seat, named for Governor Joseph McMinn. The county is named for the early American patriot, General Joseph Warren, who fell at the Battle of Bunker Hill.

McMinnville lies in the "Piedmont" section of the Cumberlands, surrounded by a chain of green hills. Beyond the hills the blue ridge of the Cumberlands and long, jagged backbone of Walden's Ridge are a lure to the traveler. There is no more beautiful way to "cross over the mountain" than through Spencer and Pikeville. It is rugged, lonely country.

The great ridge of Cumberland Mountain rises just to the east, and under Cardwell Mountain, a timbered ridge detached from the high plateau, lies Cumberland Caverns.

The cave is about six miles east of town. Signs point the way, and despite its rather isolated location, Cumberland Caverns has been doing well as a tourist attraction.

The cave was discovered in 1810 by Aaron Higgenbotham and for many years was known as Higgenbotham's Cave. It was said that the discoverer got lost in the vast cavern when his torch went out. He was rescued some days later—and, as the story goes, his hair turned white during the ordeal.

During the War of 1812 and the Civil War, the cave was mined for saltpeter, which is used in the manufacture of gunpowder. In 1948 serious explorations were begun by members of the National Speleological Society. Many of the young speleologists, or spelunkers (sportsmen rather than scientific explorers), were from Nashville. Roy Davis, a student at David Lipscomb in Nashville, and Tom Barr, Jr., were among the group. Another Nashvillian, Burt Denton, Jr., had to strip off his clothing to squeeze through the Onyx Curtain entrance, which he discovered.

In 1953 Davis and a group of explorers discovered the "Meatgrinder" entrance which connected Cumberland with the old Henshaw Cave. This led directly into the large "rooms" or caverns and made it possible to open the cave on a commercial basis.

The owners of Cumberland Caverns refer to it as America's second largest cave (second only to Mammoth) and one of the "wonders of the world." While only about a half mile of the cavern's passage and rooms are open to the public, under the mountain there is a vast network of passages, fifteen miles in length, which have been charted by young explorers. This so-called "Great Extension" of the cave, never seen by the public, contains beautiful gypsum "flowers" extruding from the ceilings. In these dark passages, too, stands the eighteen-foot Monument Pillar, pure white, with a pool of green water at its base.

The commercial section of the cave has been improved by youngsters working on a shoestring. It has sawdust trails, concealed lights, and wooden steps. The trip through the cave requires about an hour and a half. Temperature inside the cave is always fifty-six degrees, regardless of outside weather. It never rains, of course, and the seventy-five foot layer of rock over the cavern does not leak, making a "dry" cave. This is a relative term, since humidity is ninety-nine percent. There are eight waterfalls in the caverns, one of them eighty feet high. The water generally lies in pools and disappears in the bowels of the earth.

An underground dining room has been developed in one of the caverns, where large groups are sometimes served by a restaurant in McMinnville. Acoustics are perfect, and a stage has been fitted up for dramatic and musical programs. The biggest thing in the cavern is the vast "Hall of the Mountain King," 600 feet across, 140 feet high, and 150 feet wide. In ages past huge rocks have fallen to the floor of this mighty cavern, making it impossible to see it all at one time. But it is still an imposing cavern—the largest in any Southeastern cave.

Beyond the great hall, or perhaps in its last section, is the "Cathedral," a magnificent display of cave formations. Here a program called "Creation" is given with lighting and sound effects, leaving visitors with thoughts to ponder. There is a moment of darkness during this program which demonstrates that nowhere is darkness so pitch black as in the heart of a great cave.

By the Shellsford Road it is only a few miles to Highway 30, which leads to Spencer and Fall Creek Falls State Park. Here the road runs in a trough between two high ridges, called Laurel Cove.

Eleven miles from Spencer is an area of nearly sixteen thousand acres—Fall Creek Falls State Park. Perhaps it should have been named for Cane Creek, as Fall Creek Falls is only one of a number of spectacular waterfalls into the gulf or canyon of Cane Creek.

The park lies on the Cumberland Plateau. The tumbling waters of Cane Creek have cut a gulf into the rocky highland—a "grand canyon" which at some places is a mile wide and six hundred feet deep. A number of creeks "fall" into the Cane Creek gorge from the top of the plateau, creating a series of spectacular and musical waterfalls, tumbling, and cascading down the rocky sides of the canyon into "plunge pools" of deep blue water.

Highest of the falls into Cane Creek is the famous Fall Creek Falls, which drops 256 feet into a shaded plunge pool. This is a hundred feet higher than Niagara Falls, but the volume of water is only a trickle compared to the mighty cataract. Other falls on the Cane Creek include Rock House Creek, 125 feet, and Pine Creek, with a sheer drop of 85 feet.

Since there are two land levels in the park, the top of the plateau and the gulf of Cane Creek, there are two distinct types of forests. The oak-hickory forest is on the upper level, and in the gulf is found a yellow-poplar-hemlock forest. This lower level forest includes laurel, rhododendron, witch hazel, ironwood, and species of magnolia. To be in this forest below Fall Creek is a delightful experience.

The scenery along Cumberland Mountain leads me to the conclusion that excitement lies in variety and contrast—where the water splashes on rocky shores, and the mountain meets the plain.

Blue water does meet the plain—or rather the steep hills—at Center Hill Lake on the Caney Fork. Smithville lies at the front door of the lake. Center Hill is one of Tennessee's most beautiful lakes, with scores of inlets, coves, and hollows. Steep, wooded hills along the shoreline are dotted with cottages and boat docks. The lake is a favorite for fishermen from all over the state.

THE LONG BLUE LINE

The moon is there, as former President Kennedy said. So is Cumberland Mountain. Remote, challenging, but ever the same. The Blue Ridge of Middle Tennessee, Cumberland Mountain, has been looking down on the Basin and the Highland Rim since the memory of man. "That long, level blue line," Mary Murfree called it, "in which the converging mountains meet."

Cumberland Mountain is part of a great plateau reaching

91

from southern New York to central Alabama. It is the western escarpment of this plateau, where the blue line rises from the Highland Rim in rocky bluffs and wooded ridges, that Middle Tennesseans call Cumberland Mountain.

Cumberland Mountain rises about a thousand feet above the Highland Rim, fifteen hundred feet above Nashville, and two thousand feet above the sea. Some high ridges reach three thousand feet—half the altitude of the towering Smokies, but still quite mountainous to Middle Tennessee lowlanders.

In spring and early summer the mountains, like the rivers and lakes, are at their best. Colors are not as bright as at first frost, but ridges are green, gray, and blue, changing with the weather and the time of day.

"Buried in the bosom of this plateau," says an old account, "are huge treasures of coal and iron." This is true, but the treasure has been a mixed blessing. Harry Caudill, a recent writer on the Cumberland Mountain country, points out that mountains have been skinned and decapitated in the search for coal, their once-wooded crests left in heaps of slag and rubble.

"Coal has always cursed the land in which it lies," wrote Caudill. "When men begin to wrest it from the earth it leaves a legacy of foul streams, hideous slag heaps, and polluted air."

There are no coal mines in evidence, however, when the traveler toward Manchester approaches the mountain. First comes the Highland Rim, rising sharply just south of the little village of Noah. Manchester, then, lies on the Rim and in sight of the mountain. Eight miles down the road toward Monteagle the road to Viola runs off to the left, passing green, level farms which boast of wheat fields and fat cattle, and to the south and east runs the blue-green line of Cumberland Mountain.

At Hillsboro, where the road turns off to Viola, Bert Garrison, a feed salesman for many years in the mountain country, said, "I've been traveling around these hills for years and I can tell you there are changes taking place on the mountain. Coal mining and lumbering used to be the big things on the mountain, but now they don't amount to so much. People are returning to agriculture. The plateau soil responds to fertilizer, and people are making good crops of cabbage, corn, and beans.

"There's one thing about this country I don't understand," Garrison said thoughtfully. "I don't see why spring water down here on the Rim would be colder than it is on the Mountain. But it is, for a fact.

"As for the mountain people, I don't think they're any different from those of us who live on the Rim. It used to be that people down here had better educational opportunities, but with consolidated schools that's not the case now. Good roads and television have pulled people closer together, made them more alike in their tastes, habits, and ways of living."

Not far from the pleasant rural community of Viola, is the old Cumberland Academy, now a church. The face of the mountain is just east of there, and from it projects a spur which divides the watershed of Duck River, to the south and west, from the waters of the Caney Fork, to the north.

Cumberland Mountain is noted for towering crags and massive bluffs, for thundering waterfalls and dark caves that send long fissures deep into the heart of the mountain. But it is not these "spectaculars" that have won the hearts of singers and poets. The twin symbols of the mountain that have captured most space in Tennessee literature are quieter and more subdued. They are Ben Lomond Mountain, just outside McMinnville, and Lost Creek in White County.

The most prolific writers to describe the plateau and its people were two Murfreesboro girls who fell in love with the bluffs and coves. Neither of them ever married but devoted their lives to their work. They were Mary N. Murfree, who wrote under the name of Charles Egbert Craddock, and Will Allen Dromgoole. Miss Dromgoole's novel *The Sunny Side of the Cumberland* was shyly published under the name of Will Allen.

Mary Murfree wrote of her heroine, Cynthia Ware:

"Even Lost Creek itself, meandering for miles between the ranges, suddenly sinks into the earth, tunnels an unknown channel beneath the mountain, and is never seen again. She came to fancy that her life . . . was drifting down Lost Creek, to vanish vaguely in the mountains.

"There was a time—and she remembered it well—when she saw only a stream, gaily wandering down the valley, with the

laurel and the pawpaw close to its banks and the killdee's nest
in the sand."

Will Allen's light-hearted *Sunny Side* has chapters to beckon
the reader. There is "On to Sparta," "Hero of the Calf Killer,"
"The Old Stage Stand—Beckwith's," and "The Legend of Sunset
Rock."

Miss Dromgoole's *Highland City* was certainly McMinnville,
and her descriptions of Ben Lomond show that her heroine was
staying at the old Sedberry Hotel. She wrote:

"From a third-story window we looked toward Ben Lomond.
The pine summit is still wrapped in a dense, massive looking
vapor. While we watch, the vapor begins to rise like a vast black
shadow, leaving the lower mountain bright and green and beautiful." And later: "The sun casts a long glint of golden light
upon the pine plumes of Ben Lomond."

In 1874 Joseph B. Killebrew described Ben Lomond in more
practical terms:

"Chief of the spurs is Ben Lomond, an arm of the Tableland
embracing the valley of Collins River. It branches out from
the Tableland near the southern boundary (of Warren County)
and extends northward for about twelve miles, terminating in
a bold peak which commands one of the finest of the many
extended and beautiful views that may be seen from many points
on the escarpment of the Tableland."

Writing of McMinnville, Killebrew added: "On the south
looms up Ben Lomond, densely covered with trees, with only
here and there a diminutive field that looks like a dark shadow
resting upon a sea of emerald where some mountaineer, loving
the upper air, is exacting contributions from its fertile sides."

The railroad to Sparta was new when Will Allen Droomgoole,
in the guise of her heroine, Nell Courtney, rode the iron rails.
She deplored the passing of the old stage road—"its travel gone
to enrich the coffers of the iron track. Gone the glory of the
stage days, the crack of the driver's whip, the rumble of the
old vehicle; the music of the horn that used to wind down the
mountain passes has died into an echo, heard only in the memory
of the old grandfather or grandmother, dreaming while the
shadows are lengthening."

She could not foresee, in those years, the coming of the automobile, the smooth highway, and the decline of the railroad—at least in its passenger-carrying division. The old taverns are now motels.

The first man to settle in Warren County was Elisha Pepper, who lived to a ripe old age—and lived up to his name. He bitterly opposed the railroad built from Tullahoma to McMinnville in 1858 and extended to Sparta in later years. "The old man was so mad," wrote historian W. T. Hale, "that it is said he would never look at a train; for years he nursed his wrath to keep it warm."

The highway winds north to Sparta, and east of the town, across the Caney Fork, rises the mountain. A new road climbs to Bon Air, once a well-known mountain resort, and that is as good a place as any to climb Cumberland Mountain.

Near the top the road widens out for a parking place beside a rocky bluff. Below lies the valley, Sparta, and the Caney Fork—a view worth the climb. More than words can do, it tells the story of Cumberland Mountain.

GRASSY COVE

Geologists refer to it as a limestone sink. A poet has called it the gem of Cumberland Mountain. But Fred Powell, livestock specialist at the University of Tennessee, has perhaps the best and simplest description of Grassy Cove, in Cumberland County:

"It's a beautiful valley," Powell said. "There's nothing else like it in the state."

It's true there is richer soil in the delta country. There are higher peaks in the Smokies. But it's in Grassy Cove that mountain and plain come together, and the land lies as pretty as you please. Grassy Cove is actually a landlocked sea of grass, dotted by fat Angus cattle, entirely surrounded by mountains. In the shape of a stretched bow, the cove lies between Crab Orchard Mountain and Walden's Ridge. It is five miles long and two miles to eighty rods wide.

The valley floor contains 3,880 acres, most of it in grain crops, hay, and pasture to feed the cattle. There are twenty-seven families living in Grassy Cove, according to farmer-storekeeper John Kemmer, including six families of Kemmers. Some of the families have been living there for more than a century and a half, since the earliest settlers came to Cumberland County.

The Kemmer families own about half the land in the cove, and another member of the family also owns a general store. There is one church in the valley, the Grassy Cove Methodist Church. The school has been closed, and the children now go by bus to the Homestead consolidated elementary school and the high school in Crossville.

Red, green, and black are primary colors in the cove, with

97

substantial brick farm homes, barns painted dark red, and the black Aberdeen Angus silhouetted against green fields and mountain slopes. The floor of Grassy Cove is three hundred feet below the surface of the Tableland of Cumberland Mountain. Cove Creek, the one stream which drains the valley, can find no other way out but through a cave under the mountain, at the western edge of the cove. At times, during big rains, the underground passage can't handle all the water, and the valley floor is covered with water.

One former resident put it this way. "You could put a load of hay in that cave and it would be like putting a plug in the drain of a bathtub. The cove would just fill up."

About five miles from the cave where Cove Creek disappears under the mountain, it reappears as a "Big Spring" to form the Sequatchie River, at the head of the Sequatchie Valley. The spring here is about five hundred feet lower than the point where the creek ran under the mountain. In the days before the Civil War, a big grist mill stood where Cove Creek runs into the mountain. The mills in the Sequatchie Valley had to depend on this millpond for water, and often they'd send up word to "throw a few buckets of water over the dam so's we can grind."

For many generations Grassy Cove has been the pride of Cumberland Mountain for its beauty and fertility, the rugged plateau country having not too much to offer along this line. And the cove is still rich enough, John Kemmer points out, for a man to make a living from the soil.

While a young man can bring up his family in the cove if he owns land, the hard fact is that the land is limited, fenced in by mountains. As a result there aren't very many young folks in the cove. Total population is estimated by Kemmer at around 160. About six hundred head of Angus cattle and a few Herefords graze under trees beside Cove Creek.

Grassy Cove was hit hard by the Civil War. Family ties were broken as the young men joined up with both armies. After the war, however, the post office was reopened and prosperity gradually returned. Soon after the war a Northern capitalist, Lorenzo Stratton of New York, bought eighteen-hundred acres in Grassy Cove and settled his family there. Stratton built a new saw and grist mill on the creek, planted trees, operated a small nursery, and introduced a fine herd of Devon cattle into the cove. His farm became a showplace, as much admired on the mountain as was Belle Meade plantation in the Central Basin.

Only the old people in the cove remember the Devons now—they have long since given way to the Angus, pride of the Kemmer family, but it is generally agreed that they were small, red, short-horned cattle, an English-bred dual purpose breed. The Strattons, too, are gone, but Cora and Nettie Stratton, as artists and poets, added to the cultural heritage of Grassy Cove. The trees they planted still shade the George Kemmer home, and the little history of Grassy Cove they wrote is a valuable and rare source of information.

Why is Grassy Cove so special? What does it have that other mountain coves are lacking? Perhaps it's a combination of things: scenery, with surrounding peaks rising five hundred to a thousand feet above the fields, fine cattle, and well-tended farms. The soil is good, but it has been tilled for many generations and must be built up with a complete fertilizer.

"One advantage we've got here," said George Kemmer, "is the rainy showers in summertime. If it rains anywhere, it'll rain on the mountain."

Like other things in this world, the cove is not quite perfect. There's an automobile junkyard right in the heart of it. While climbing the mountain to take a last look at the valley, however, one must conclude that the green cove is a mighty pretty dimple on the face of Cumberland Mountain—a pastoral retreat that no country or continent can surpass.

From Clarkrange, south of Jamestown, a lonely rural road runs across the plateau to Monterey, once called Standing Stone. The place was named originally for two "standing stones" which the first white men found by the trail—according to early tradition. Historian Alvin Wirt says the stones were not very large and were evidently set by human hands. He adds that charcoal was found in the ground under the stones.

One of the stones was about a foot square and several feet

high, Wirt reports, and what remained of this stone was mounted on a monument, just off the highway in Monterey, by the Improved Order of Red Men. Standing Stone State Park takes its name from this landmark. The inscription says it is called *Neeya-Kah-Ohkel,* or Standing Stone.

Monterey is said to have been given its name by an engineer on the Tennessee Central Railroad, perhaps for "mountain-girt" Monterey, capital of the Mexican state of Nuevo Leon and scene of a great battle of the Mexican War.

In his *Upper Cumberland of Pioneer Times* Wirt wrote that "Forks of the Road," later called Mount Granger, was located near the Putnam County village of Brotherton, also on the Tennessee Central Railroad. Here the historic Cumberland Turnpike divided into the Walton Road and the Fort Blount Branch Road—"a spot designated as the western distribution point for all mails to the Southwestern frontiers." Wirt also locates the fork about four and a half miles east of Algood.

THE CANE-GUN BATTLE

A hundred and fifty years ago boys on the Tennessee frontier had no missiles or merry-go-rounds—but did you ever hear of a cane-gun musket?

Joe Bishop of Smith County, Tennessee, was an old man in 1857 when he told the story of his life to John W. Gray. Gray wrote a book about it, and *The Life of Joe Bishop* (1858) contains the only known account of a cane-gun battle.

Back in Indian days, historians say, all the creek beds and lowlands of the back country were covered with waving green cane, ten to twenty feet high. Herds of buffalo crashed through the cane making trails to springs and salt licks. Indians and animals skulked and hunted in the cane, and for cows and calves it was the staff of life.

From the cane we got such historic names as "Caney Fork River," and the never to be forgotten remark of a Confederate soldier at Nashville: "The rattling of fifty caliber rifles sounded like a canebrake on fire."

Young Joe Bishop's cane gun was made of stern stuff. Finding a cane of the right length and diameter, he loaded it with a charge of gunpowder and a lead ball, or smooth round pebble. To fire it off, he applied a coal of fire!

How did young Joe spend his time with this old-fashioned, bullet-firing cap pistol? Let him tell his own story:

"A neighbor boy and myself, in the absence of other mischief, agreed that while one of us should represent a wild deer, the other should act as the huntsman and shoot at him with the cane gun.

101

"We repaired to the forest, and after a few minutes over preliminaries, I induced him to let me act the deer first and he take the first shot, I having a special inclination to take a crack at him last.

"The terms now being understood, he loaded the cane gun with powder and one shot, and prepared a chunk of fire with which to touch her off.

"I about this time went away into the bushes and lay down, and jumped up as though a pack of yelling hounds had suddenly come upon me, and upon all fours came running past the hunter's stand.

"He waited until I reached a point directly opposite the stand and fired, and to my utter astonishment, he so effectually knocked me down that I thought of taking the last privilege that belongs to living things, or, in other words, making my last kick.

"In reality I knew not but that I was mortally wounded. His shot had struck me just behind the shoulder, raising a knot upon one of my ribs fully as large as a partridge egg, and while I tumbled and scringed and writhed as though a firebrand had been pressed against me for the time—for it stung most intolerably—he turned pale and shuddered as if the icy fangs of death were closing around his heart.

"This cured us of this kind of sport; for a while the very thought of the cane gun threw him into an immediate nervous trepidation, regarding them, as he now did, as sharpshooters. I had no disposition, on the other hand, to kill him, an event which previous to my being shot I had never apprehended."

Sounds properly apprehensive, doesn't he? But how long do you think young Joe stayed cured? Two pages later:

"Upon one occasion we manufactured after our own fashion, a supply of cane muskets; we loaded them with powder and one shot in each, to be discharged by the chunk of fire, all the same as in the deer hunt, except this time we took the precaution to extend the distance from eight to thirty yards."

As luck would have it, after much firing between the contending armies, Joe shot his old adversary "on the front of the thigh just above the knee.

"He laid hold of the limb with both hands, limped round, and bellowed to such a frightful degree, that the battle was at once lost and won, the victory mine."

It would be pleasant to relate that Joe reformed after this engagement, but he only transferred the scene of his sport from land to water.

"At another time," the account continues, "we constructed ships out of cornstalks, manned them with so many cannons formed of cane, and launched them upon the deep waters of a tan vat."

These adventures were but the beginning, and Joe Bishop never did settle down. He became a famous scout and hunter, and later a peace officer somewhat on the order of Wyatt Earp. The people in his part of Middle Tennessee still remember the name—Joe Bishop—with respect.

And there's a cheering note for harried parents. Joe died peacefully in bed, of the rigors of time and old age, full of years and honors.

Buttermilk Spring, where
Jackson, his boots full of
blood from the wound Dickinson
gave him, stopped to rest.

THE DUELING GROUND

The time was seven o'clock on the morning of May 30, 1806. The place was in the "second bottom" of the Red River, two and a half miles west of Adairville, Kentucky. Two men faced each other, exactly twenty-four feet apart, each standing by a peg that had been driven in the ground to mark his position.

The younger man wore light gray trousers and a powder blue coat. The other, nearing middle age, was dressed in dark blue. Both men looked grim and determined. Each had in his right hand a nine-inch dueling pistol, loaded with a one-ounce lead ball.

Thomas Overton spoke. "Gentlemen, are you ready?"

"Ready," replied Charles Dickinson.

"Yes, sir," said Andrew Jackson.

"FIRE," shouted Overton.

Sun glinted on steel as Dickinson's pistol came up and almost instantly fired.

There was a little puff of dust from his coat as the big bullet hit Jackson in the chest. He put his left hand over the spot, steadied himself, and raised his pistol.

Inadvertently, Dickinson stepped back from his peg. "Great God," he exclaimed, "have I missed him?"

"Back to the mark, sir!" shouted Overton, presenting his own pistol.

Dickinson stepped back to his peg, averted his eyes, and waited.

Jackson raised his pistol, aimed, and pulled the trigger. There was a light click as the hammer stopped at half-cock.

105

The suspense seemed unbearable.

Jackson cocked his pistol, drew another bead and fired. Dickinson fell, his life's blood staining his trousers.

For a generation men discussed every detail of the encounter which cost Dickinson his life. People came from miles around to see the "dueling ground" in the years before the Civil War. Today the duel is almost forgotten. Few have seen the spot where Jackson sent Dickinson to his grave.

Hal Angel now lives in the house where Dickinson died of his wound hours after the duel. It was then known as Harrison's Tavern and stands on the bank of Red River.

The neat farmhouse has asbestos shingles covering its ancient logs, and the casual passer-by would hardly guess its historical associations.

It was Joe Angel, a twelve-year-old boy, who pointed out the big sycamore tree where Dickinson's bearers laid the wounded man to rest on the way up to the house from the river bottom, and he pointed out the little upstairs room where the young man died, asking at the last—"Why have you turned out the lights?"

Miller's Tavern, where Jackson had a fried chicken dinner and slept soundly the night before the duel, is perhaps a mile from Harrison's Tavern and across the river.

Near Miller's, now owned by Jim Rutherford of Adairville, is the famous Buttermilk Spring where Jackson, his boots full of blood from the wound Dickinson gave him, stopped to rest on the way back to the tavern.

Jackson saw a woman churning at the spring, and she gave him a glass of buttermilk. The spring has not changed to this day, and still sends a powerful stream into Red River.

On the beautiful farm owned by O. F. Boyd, formerly called the Jeff Burr place, is the site where the duel was fought, and a line tree marks the approximate spot where the duelers stood.

The duel came about after an exchange of insults between Jackson and Dickinson over a horse race wager and loose remarks made by Dickinson concerning Jackson's wife. The matter was further aggravated by a young man named Swann, who

became involved over a forfeit posted by Dickinson after with-
drawing his horse from a race with Jackson's "Truxton."

Dickinson's bullet had fractured Jackson's ribs, and he was
confined to his bed for a month. Then the wound healed
"falsely." Jackson's biographer, Parton, thought the Dickinson
wound eventually caused his death.

As for young Charles Dickinson he was buried on the Peach
Blossom plantation owned by his father-in-law, James Erwin.
Years later his son returned and erected a tomb over the spot—
and a picture of this tomb is to be found in Mrs. James Caldwell's
Beautiful and Historic Homes Around Nashville. Today the
tomb is gone, and there is no sign to mark the grave of the
man who lies buried in the front lawn of a house at 216 Carden
Avenue, Nashville.

MAMMOTH CAVE BY LANTERN LIGHT

"The Lantern Tour is special and unique," according to a leaflet from Mammoth Cave. Guide John Hill explained that the lantern tour was experimental. It was intended to recapture something of the romance and adventure of "caving" of a century ago, before the advent of electric lighting.

"A crowd of people walking through a well-lighted cave makes it look like a shopping center," an observer said. "With lanterns and torches we see the cave as prehistoric men saw it—and that's how a cave ought to be seen."

The lantern tour goes through an old part of the cave, unlighted and not shown to the public for the last twenty-five years. It lasts three hours, covers three miles, and for its duration the party guides are out of touch with the surface.

"This is a strenuous tour with some steep grades," Hill warns every party. "Anybody with heart symptoms or other trouble can back out now and get his money back."

The tour begins at the Violet City man-made entrance and the "steep grades" begin almost at once. Persons making this tour are advised to wear rubber soled shoes.

All are admonished to stick to the trail—a two hundred pound man with a sprained ankle deep in a cave can present a problem. At times the guide stops to tell something of the history of the cavern, explaining that the great limestone rocks were deposited by an inland sea many millions of years ago. The action of water made great fissures and seams in the rocks, which had been thrust upward by some interior force.

109

In time the nearby Green River, cutting an ever deeper channel, lowered the water table, leaving the great, rocky passages
high and dry—the Mammoth Cave we see today.

The cave was discovered in 1798 by a man chasing a wounded
bear, but it had been known to prehistoric people thousands
of years before. It was established as a national park in 1941.
Some caves are considered more beautiful than Mammoth, but
none is more impressive. It has long been considered one of
the Seven Wonders of the World and for centuries was thought
to be the world's largest cave.

The bobbing lantern but dimly lights the passages as a party
winds its way through the caverns. And the guides put on an
exhibition that astonishes everyone. They swirl an oil-soaked
torch around their heads, then throw it high and far, like a
shooting star, across the blackness to a small high ledge. The
burning torch lights up rock formations at the roof of the cavern.
This performance is repeated several times during the lantern
tour.

Hill explained that the guides often threw torches a hundred
years ago, but the practice was discontinued when most of the
cave was lighted. He and his partner are trying to equal the
skill of the old guides as torch throwers.

The Star Chamber, drawn by A. R. Waud in 1871, is impressive
as ever, and it is here that the lighted part of the cave begins.
The Giant's Coffin, Lover's Leap, and Underground River are
some of the more popular sights in the cave. A cave is a record
of natural history and the history of man, historic and prehistoric. Mammoth, like every other cave, has a personality of its
own. It even breathes, like some hibernating monster, heaving
out cool air in summer and warm air (relatively speaking) in
winter. The interior is well-ventilated and is always a cool
fifty-four degrees.

One of the most interesting items in Mammoth Cave is the
Indian "mummy." Twenty-four hundred years ago a prehistoric
man of the Adena culture entered the cave to mine gypsum—why
these ancient people wanted the gypsum we do not know. The
kneeling gypsum miner chipped away at a rock and loosened
a five-ton boulder that crushed him to death. His body was

preserved by the constant temperature and humidity of the cave, and in 1935 his "mummy" was found. Chain hoists were used to lift the boulder, and today the little man can be seen in a glass case, along with woven sandals and other artifacts of these early people. The man lies in the crumpled position of defeat and death, just as he was crushed by the great rock. He seems to represent humanity, defeated and crushed by forces he could not understand or control. After the centuries, there were other men who could lift the stone.

The modern history of Mammoth Cave is almost as interesting as its ancient history. The nitrate works built during the War of 1812 are still there—without them Andrew Jackson might not have won the Battle of New Orleans. The engineering of these workmen was of a high order. Using metal-capped wooden augers they bored out the centers of poplar poles and expertly fitted them together to make pipelines half a mile long from the mouth of the cave to the works.

Two grim stone huts in the cave tell the pathetic story of a young doctor who brought tuberculosis patients to live in the cave, hoping to cure them of the dread disease. Most of them died, including the doctor himself, in a pitiful attempt to conquer an unknown enemy.

Huge as the cave is, it cannot be seen or understood in one tour, and people with spelunking tendencies will want to make more. The lantern tour, with its flaming torches, catches something of the excitement of cave exploring, and is likely to grow in public favor.

While the cave is the centerpiece, there are other attractions in Mammoth Cave National Park. A visitor center and souvenir shop are popular with the five thousand people who visit the park each day. The concessions include a comfortable motel built over the cave—but reservations should be made in advance. Other activities include hiking on nature trails and scenic boat trips on Green River.

At Bardstown, which is not far from Mammoth Cave, is the Old Barton distillery, now the "Whiskey Museum of America." It has paintings, pictures, and bottles reminiscent of the turbulent times of John Barleycorn. There are rare bottles of many shapes—a "Booz" bottle which gave booze its name, a hatchet-shaped Carrie Nation bottle, and a bottle especially made for the GAR (Union Army) reunion of 1895.

"When the Moon Comes Over the Mountain" was a cartoon drawn by a Tennessee cartoonist now with the Chicago *Tribune*. With high taxes going higher on whiskey, an old moonshiner is furbishing up his equipment and making for the hills, to resume his business at the same old stand as during prohibition.

"What's Your Pleasure, Mr. President?" was a drawing loaned the museum by Esquire Corp. It showed many Presidents—perhaps all of them—giving their answers to the question. Here are some:

Lyndon Johnson—"A little scotch in moderation."

Harry Truman—"Bourbon and branch water."

James K. Polk—"I don't drink."

John Kennedy—"A daiquiri, thank you."

Andrew Johnson—"Tennessee whiskey by choice."

Dwight Eisenhower—"To the best of my knowledge I like Coke."

In Bardstown is the beautiful St. Joseph's Cathedral, built in 1816, the first Catholic Cathedral west of the Alleghenies.

Across town is "My Old Kentucky Home," where the music of Stephen Foster fills the air. It was here that the young composer got an inspiration for "My Old Kentucky Home." An outdoor drama, "The Stephen Foster Story" is a big attraction in this truly beautiful Kentucky town.

South, on highway 31-E, is the national park which preserves the "traditional" log cabin where Abe Lincoln was born. The cabin was shown at expositions around the country, including the Tennessee Centennial at Nashville in 1897. It's a little smaller than it originally was and is enclosed in a marble temple.

The countryside of southern Kentucky is a reminder of the surface beauty of the world, the deaths of the ancient miner and Floyd Collins, and the fame and tragedy that came to Abe Lincoln.

GRANDEUR IN NASHVILLE

Nashville on the Cumberland started out in a rude log fort. It was a plain heritage—but today the city can boast of many beautiful homes—some of them famous and open to the public as museum houses.

The Hermitage

Like a great lodestone set among tall cedars, the Hermitage draws visitors from all across America, people who have heard of the name and fame of Andrew Jackson. The Tennessee farmer who became the hero of New Orleans and seventh president of the United States sleeps in the garden beside his beloved wife, Rachel, but Hermitage Director James Arnold says that the spirit of Jackson is not dead—his presence can still be felt at the Hermitage.

The Hermitage is a preservation—and to some extent a restoration—of the home of Jackson. The furniture, the clothing, the books, the guns, and the paintings—everything that was part of life at the Hermitage in Jackson's day is in its place. But there is constant change there. In recent years, Tulip Grove—the home of Andrew Jackson Donelson and his wife, Emily—has been restored and is operated as a separate site across Lebanon Road. The church where Jackson worshiped has been restored near Tulip Grove. It was dedicated in May, 1969, and opened to the public. Jackson's carriage, too, has been restored and returned to the Hermitage grounds.

113

The Hermitage—Photo courtesy Tennessee Conservation Department.

The Hermitage is the most popular historic shrine in Tennessee, but had it not been for the efforts of the Ladies' Hermitage Association, it very likely wouldn't be here. For a time it seemed it would become a U.S. military academy—the West Point of the West. And there was a time when the Hermitage seemed destined to become an Old Soldiers' Home for Confederate veterans.

It was touch and go, for Tennessee was Southern—and Jackson had been considered a national man. John Berrien Lindsley said: "It was not Grant at the head of his enormous columns, not Lincoln in his chair at Washington; it was the soul of Jackson, who said, 'The Federal Union must and shall be preserved,' that defeated us in the War of the States. . . . Tennessee should have taken care of the veterans, but the Hermitage should be preserved forever."

The veterans were given their home on the property—and it has long since disappeared. But the Hermitage is still here, close to the heart of Tennessee and America.

Travellers' Rest

Architectural "detectives" are still in the process of historic restoration at Travellers' Rest. The house is in a new phase of a fifteen-year restoration of the mansion to what it was back in 1828, when Judge John Overton, a friend and political adviser of General Andrew Jackson, was its owner. Travellers' Rest is operated as a museum house by the Society of Colonial Dames in Tennessee. In the "History Room" is a delicate little green wineglass, presented by the Ladies' Hermitage Association. From this glass the Marquis de Lafayette drank a toast when he visited Nashville in 1825 as the "guest of the nation."

The house was built on top of an Indian mound. Prehistoric or Stone Grave Indians lived in the vicinity, and in the early days the plantation was called Golgotha, meaning "Place of the Skull." A collection of skeletons and artifacts of these early Indians is on display.

The mansion is a growth, and the sections have been seen

Travellers' Rest—Photo courtesy Tennessee Conservation Department.

as interpreting the course of Tennessee and American history. As tastes and skills changed with the times, from Indian days to the cotton economy of the 1840s and 1850s, the house grew larger and more luxurious. A former president of the Dames, Mrs. Andrew Benedict, has called the house a "textbook in Tennessee history."

During the Battle of Nashville in December, 1864, Travellers' Rest served as headquarters for General John B. Hood, commander of the Confederate Army of Tennessee.

Belle Meade

Belle Meade has been called the Queen of Southern Plantations. At 110 Leake Avenue, Nashville, facing Harding Road, the farm was once a way station on the Natchez Trace, according to director Richard H. Hulan. The beautiful Greek

Restoring a wheel at the Belle Meade Carriage Museum.

Belle Meade Mansion—Photo courtesy Tennessee Conservation Department.

revival mansion with twenty-four acres of land is the property
of the Association for the Preservation of Tennessee Antiquities.

Belle Meade (the name means "beautiful meadow") was
founded in 1807 by John Harding. His son, General William
G. Harding, was born in the log cabin which still stands on
the lawn, one of the oldest buildings in Middle Tennessee.

At the turn of the century, the plantation was the leading
thoroughbred stud farm in the United States. Two of its most
famous horses were Enquirer and Iroquois. Iroquois was the
first American horse to win the English Derby. The carriage
house, built just prior to the introduction of automobiles, is
bigger than the mansion itself. The carriage collection contains
four vehicles belonging to the Harding and Jackson families,
who owned Belle Meade, and twenty others donated by interested individuals.

Bullets flew at Belle Meade during the 1864 Battle of Nashville, and their marks can still be seen on the classic columns.
A daughter of the family, Selene Harding, refused to go in the
house and remained on the porch to wave at Confederate soldiers. She later married one of them, Colonel William H. Jackson.

Cheekwood

On a hill overlooking Belle Meade, just off Highway 100,
stands the vine-covered, gray stone Georgian mansion, Cheekwood. A winding driveway leads from Cheek Road past the wild
flower garden in its natural setting; and then around the magnificent boxwood to the large double doors of the house.

The sixty-room mansion was built in 1929 by Mr. and Mrs.
Leslie Cheek, whose family founded the Maxwell House coffee
firm. The Cheeks and their architect, Bryant Fleming, traveled
extensively in England collecting art treasures for the 18th
century style home. The two-story entry hall, with its marble
floor and curving stairway, sets the mood for the entire house.
Elegant and graceful, Cheekwood is so well-proportioned that
it never seems "big" or "overdone," but simply gracious.

Cheekwood

In 1957 Mr. and Mrs. Walter Sharp, daughter and son-in-law of Leslie Cheek, gave the house and surrounding fifty acres to the Nashville community to be used as a combination fine arts center, arboretum, and botanical garden. The third floor was converted to an art gallery, with space for a permanent exhibit and special showings.

In 1969 Wildings wild flower garden was moved from its site in east Nashville to a hillside spot near the Cheekwood driveway.

Although a tour of the house is a rewarding experience, Cheekwood is not a museum house. It is used as an educational and entertainment center. Lectures, movies, exhibits, flower shows, nature hikes, art classes, and workshops of all kinds may be found in the schedule of events. It is truly a cultural center.

Left: The Grand Old Opry House, once called the Ryman Auditorium. Below: The Country Music Hall of Fame at the corner of Sixteenth Avenue South and Division Street.
—Photos courtesy the Tennessee Conservation Department.

SEE AND REMEMBER

Grand Ole Opry House

At the Grand Ole Opry House on Opry Place (Fifth Avenue) Opry lovers line up three and four abreast waiting to see their favorite show.

The Opry House was built in 1892 with contributions from the people of Nashville. Captain Tom Ryman, who operated a line of steamboats on the Cumberland River, gave both money and time to make the enterprise possible. He wanted Nashville to have a suitable place to hold the revival meetings so popular at that time. It was named the Union Gospel Tabernacle under a "welfare" charter. After Captain Ryman's death, the name was changed to Ryman Auditorium in his memory.

The Grand Ole Opry began appearing at the Ryman in 1941. In 1963 WSM bought the building, and it became the official home of the Grand Ole Opry, at which time the name was changed to the Grand Ole Opry House. The acoustics were always praised by artists who gave concerts there.

Country Music Hall of Fame

At the corner of 16th Avenue and Division Street is the Country Music Hall of Fame, with exhibits about the people and records that have made country music famous. There are

Children's Museum—Photo courtesy the Tennessee Conservation Department.

State Museum—Photo courtesy the Tennessee Conservation Department.

smiles and tears, memories, voices, and faces of the great stars of country music. The young face of Jimmie Rodgers looks first from the wall in the Walkway of the Stars, and brings back memories of the "Singing Brakeman" of the early days of radio.

There are many more country music greats represented by portraits in the Hall of Fame, from such men of our own time as Roy Acuff and Eddy Arnold to that great performer of other years, the Dixie Dewdrop, Uncle Dave Macon. And there is a feeling of sadness for the untimely loss of those great stars, Hank Williams and Jim Reeves.

From tapes the stars sing again, while lights focus on their pictures. Boots, fiddles, fancy pants, and cowboy hats are mementos of the great pickers and singers.

Wall displays remind of songs for every occasion:

Place songs, "Alabamy Bound"; happy songs, "You Are My Sunshine"; tragic songs, "Wreck On the Highway"; religious songs, "He's Got the Whole World in His Hand"; transportation songs, "Night Train to Memphis"; occupational songs, "Sixteen Tons"; events songs, "The Death of Floyd Collins."

Children's Museum

The Children's Museum has been called the building of happy voices, but at the end of World War II the city of Nashville was planning to tear down the building.

It was a beautiful old building that had served the University of Nashville, and it stood "near the road leading to Buchanan's Mill," as provided by the Southwest Territory in 1796.

It was saved by Historian Stanley Horn, who has saved many a landmark in his day. He told Nashville Mayor Tom Cummings, "We will find a use for that building." Men like Alfred Starr, Vernon Sharp, and Dr. Harry Vaughn put their minds and hearts to the task, and the Children's Museum was born.

It has snakes, and bright stars in its planetarium. A horse-drawn fire engine brings memories of Chief Rosetta and early

Nashville. Its wild life dioramas, art gallery, workshops, and field trips have made life better for children—and adults as well—for nearly a quarter century.

State Museum

Tennessee is called the Volunteer State because her men rushed to the colors when war came. And while the State Museum exhibits, housed in the War Memorial Building, range from prehistoric Indian artifacts to an Egyptian mummy, the central theme is war—the Revolution, Indian wars, the Civil War, World War I, World War II, and Vietnam.

Here are Ferguson's sword and sash that he lost with his life at King's Mountain and the rifle that killed him. Here is Nathan Bedford Forrest's deadly revolver and the slit boot of Southern hero Sam Davis. Here are Alvin York's medals, the automatic pistol he took from a German major, and the shotgun for which he traded a heifer. Paintings of the governors, the silver service from the battleship *Tennessee* and a Sully painting of Andrew Jackson on glass are a few among thousands of items.

THE PRIDE AND THE PAST

The pride and the past of Nashville are bound together in the old City Cemetery. Here lie the pioneers.

Without being sentimental or morbid about it, this is a good place to visit—especially for Nashvillians, for beneath this forest of old fashioned tombstones and granite boxes lies all that remains of the founders and builders who gave us the heritage of a great city—Nashville on the Bluffs.

One way to get to the cemetery is to drive from Broadway out Fourth Avenue, South. In years gone by, before some citizen, in the name of "progress," decided that streets ought to be numbered, it was called Cherry Street. Along this street, through an older section of the city, may be seen the vertical lines of crumbling "town houses," contrasting strangely with the horizontal lines of the suburban houses of today. The entrance to the cemetery is at the corner of Oak Street, through an iron gate in a sturdy stone wall.

When the City Cemetery was opened in 1822, it was well on the outskirts of the city which grew up around the public square. Today it is at the heart of a sprawling metropolis, compassed about by industry and traffic. Along the western border of the twenty-acre plot pass the tracks of the L&N Railroad, and to the east is the old station of the Nashville and Decatur Railroad. Across the tracks is St. Cloud Hill, where the Federal army built Fort Negley during the Civil War. Before the railroad came there was a Catholic cemetery on the lower slope of the hill.

In Nashville's lawless days after the war it is said that a gang

127

of thieves and bandits lived in the abandoned ruins of the fort
on the hill. These bandits were thought to have dug a tunnel
from the fort into the cemetery, coming up under the family
vault of Judge John McNairy. This pioneer judge, they thought,
had treasure buried among the bones. But as far as we know,
neither this tunnel or treasure has ever been found.

J. W. Denis wrote in the *Tennessee Historical Quarterly*
(March, 1943) that the streets in the old cemetery were named
for trees, such as Plum, Pine, Poplar, Oak, etc. Denis, who played
in the cemetery as a boy, headed the Nashville Cemetery
Commission which, with city funds, restored broken stones
and fences, repaired and lighted roads, and in many ways gave
back to the cemetery some of its pristine beauty and dignity.

There are almost forty thousand graves in the cemetery, and
most interments are now held elsewhere in the city. However,
Nashvillians who own lots are still buried there.

There are Protestants and Catholics and whites and Negroes
buried in this cemetery, and of the latter both slaves and free-
men. There is a marker in honor of Jerry Porterfield, a Negro
slave who died saving his master from the wreck of a carriage.

There are many famous people buried in the cemetery, the
most famous, perhaps, being the "Father of Middle Tennessee,"
James Robertson. Beside him and his wife, Charlotte, lies the
famous Dr. Felix Robertson, their son and the first white boy
born in Nashville. The doctor was once mayor of the city, and
it is worthy of note that nineteen other Nashville mayors are
buried in the cemetery. The grave of James Robertson's granddaughter, Tennessee, affectionately known as "Miss Tennessee,"
is one of those that has been restored by the commission.

The most famous grave in the cemetery is that of the New
England sea captain, William Driver, who designed his own
marker. The stone represents a tree trunk, entwined by flowers,
toadstools, and a frog, and embellished with a fouled anchor.
It bears this inscription:

William Driver

*A master mariner sailed twice around the world and once
around Australia, removed the Pitcairn people from sickness and*

death in Tahiti to their own island home September 3, 1821, then
69 in number, now 1200 souls. . . . His ship, his country, and
his flag, Old Glory.

It was Captain Driver who, at the Tennessee state capitol, first called the American flag "Old Glory." The Tennessee legislature has voted that the flag be flown over his grave for twenty-four hours daily under a light, and a bill to this effect was sent to the Congress of the United States.

There are two monuments in the cemetery designed by the great architect, William Strickland, who drew plans for the State Capitol and the Downtown Presbyterian Church. One of these stands by the grave of a stonemason who fell from the Capitol during construction and was killed.

There are more stones that tell sad stories of tragedy and death. The most imposing monument, paid for by the State of Tennessee, marks the grave of Governor William Carroll. But the sweetest, happiest story of all appears on the tomb of Duncan Robertson, which was paid for by the people of the city. Of him it was said: "He was the best man who ever lived in Nashville."

And what did Duncan Robertson do to earn his eulogy, and the great stone monument? The inscription tells the story:

"He gave himself, and what he had, to others."

GRANNY WHITE PIKE

All accounts have it that Granny White Pike is the most historic, the best loved, and the least changed of all the roads radiating from Nashville. It is a narrow pike, winding southward through the green Overton hills and the Harpeth Knobs.

Over the years a number of writers have turned their attention to the old pike. In 1921 C. H. Smart wrote that it was the only surviving "pike" out of Nashville, and he borrowed a line from Thomas Moore:

> *"This the last pike of Nashville*
> *Left blooming alone."*

They were all called pikes in the 1860s, Smart reported, but as new and handsome homes were built along them by the rich and the near-rich, they became Roads with a capital R.

The Granny White Pike, he continued, "with the poor and the near-poor, the black and the near-black, still retains the name pike."

Smart described the beginning of the pike at Tenth Avenue and Broadway, where the railroad now passes under the viaduct. It ran southwest, as Twelfth Avenue does now, "over the old Nashville and Chattanooga tunnel, thence past the Tennessee Asylum, on the corner of the pike and what is now Division Street." Some years ago this part of the pike was called Kayne Avenue.

In the years before 1850, the pike was called the Middle Franklin Turnpike, lying between the Franklin and Hillsboro

131

roads. It is believed to have been the first road south out of
Nashville, and was originally "engineered" by buffaloes making
a path from their Harpeth feeding grounds to the salt lick at
Nashville.

The road did go to Franklin, though not directly. In 1917
Williamson County historian Park Marshall wrote of its beginnings:

"Before (1799) there was a road from Nashville to Holly Tree
Gap along the route of what was afterwards the Granny White
Pike and a kind of woodland way thence to the place where
Franklin now stands.

"The country was a wilderness . . . with great canebrakes
and briar patches. There were many ponds and swamps and
cozy areas, for the smaller water courses were clogged with the
debris of ages.

"The (Williamson County) Court ordered a road to be cut
out from the Holly Tree Gap to Franklin. It crossed Big Harpeth
at the mouth of Spencer's Creek and came into Franklin as
the Del Rio Road now does."

Old residents along the pike have stories to tell. Farmer Ed
Fitts says fogs in the Harpeth Knobs act contrary to nature,
since they rise from the ground instead of falling from the sky.
Mrs. Howard Gardner says the fogs are just rising from the
damp valley of the Harpeth. When the tall cane grew along
the road, she says, bears came down from the Knobs to scratch
on cabin doors, looking for handouts.

Both history and present observations "bear out" Mrs.
Gardner. In the early days of the settlement at Nashville, Captain John Rains, a famous hunter, killed thirty-two bears in
one winter, most of them in the Harpeth Knobs. At the entrance
to the pass where Granny White kept her famous tavern, about
seven miles from downtown Nashville, a little cane can be found
growing to this day.

Other residents vow the hot summer sun shines in the gap
only between two and three o'clock in the afternoon, and that
the weather is a good ten degrees cooler there than in the
country around.

As Nashville's most historic trail, the Granny White Pike is connected with three great epochs of Middle Tennessee history. Going back to the beginning, it is rich in the lore and artifacts of prehistoric Stone Grave Indians who lived on Brown's Creek. The story of Granny White, who gave it her name, is one of the heartening and inspiring accounts of pioneer days. And lastly, people who lived along the pike had a front seat view of the Battle of Nashville, one of the decisive battles of the Civil War.

Historical controversies and misunderstandings have long swirled around the head of Lucinda White (folks called her Lucy), whose tavern marked the northern entrance to the gap. One cause of the misunderstandings was Thomas Hart Benton, who lived on and rode the pike. As a member of the U.S. Senate from Missouri Benton immortalized Granny White by telling her story to that body. "Let the poor get land," he said. His speech is in *Thirty Years' View.*

"The advantages of giving land to those who would settle and cultivate it was illustrated in one of my speeches by reciting the case of Granny White, well-known in her time to all the population of Middle Tennessee and especially to all those who traveled south from Nashville, along the great road which crossed the divide between the Cumberland and Harpeth waters, at the evergreen tree which gave name to the gap—the Holly Tree Gap.

"At the age of sixty she had been left a widow in the tidewater region of North Carolina. Her poverty was so extreme that when she went to the county court to get a couple of little orphan grandchildren bound to her, the justices refused to let her have them, because she could not give security to keep them off the parish.

"This compelled her to emigrate; and she set off with two little boys upon a journey of eight or nine hundred miles, to what was then called the Cumberland Settlements.

"Arrived in the neighborhood of Nashville, a generous-hearted Irishman (his name deserves to be remembered—Thomas Mc-Crory) let her have a corner of his land on her own terms—a nominal price and indefinite credit.

"It was fifty acres in extent, and comprised the two faces

of a pair of confronting hills, whose precipitous declivities lacked a few degrees, and but a few, of mathematical perpendicularity."

The long and short of Benton's story was that the old lady, staking her pumpkins to prevent their rolling out of the field, built a tavern by the road between the two hills, "for which purpose a part of the hill had to be dug away." Apparently this was unusual in a day when the clank of the bulldozer had not been heard in the land.

The old lady and her two grandchildren advanced to comparative wealth and Benton reported they had "money, slaves, horses, and cattle, and her fields extended into the valley below," and said her grandchildren were "raised up to honor and independence."

"These," Benton told the U. S. Senate, "were the fruits of economy and industry and a noble illustration of the advantage of giving land to the poor. But the federal government would have demanded sixty-two dollars and fifty cents for that land, and old Granny White and her grandchildren might have lived in misery and sunk into vice, before the opponents of this bill would have taken less."

Modern research by Mrs. Edyth Whitley of the DAR has developed that Granny White was most probably the widow of Zachariah White, killed in 1781 at the Battle of the Bluffs. A deed shows that she bought her land from Wolsey Warrington in 1803, "including the headspring of Brown's Creek," and that it had been a part of the David Beaty tract granted by North Carolina.

The conclusion is that McCrory, who is said to have killed an Indian chief with the first shot fired in the Battle of Buchanan's Station, helped Granny White secure her land, and perhaps helped her pay for it, thus winning a slightly confused tribute from Benton.

Many stories were told of the old lady, who was said to have the best brandy, the best pancakes, and the cleanest beds of any tavern on the road. One traveler, however, was displeased with the butter. He threw it to the ceiling, and it stuck there.

"You see," he said, "this is very strong butter. It sticks to the ceiling."

Another guest, it was said, became lost in the cluster of small rooms, and had to fire his pistol to bring the tavern owner to his rescue. One writer remarked that Granny was a very fine trader and managed to swap her home-grown gourds for bowls—one bowl for one gourd.

The riddle of the gaps is an enigma that has baffled a half dozen writers on the Granny White Pike. In a newspaper controversy of the 1920s historian Park Marshal held that Holly Tree Gap, frequently misspelled Hollow Tree Gap, is on the Nashville-Franklin Road in Williamson County, about four miles north of Franklin.

Champ L. Hooberry, a Nashville book dealer, contended that Holly Tree Gap was the old name for White's Gap on the Granny White Pike, seven miles south from Nashville, and that the Franklin Road gap was properly called Hollow Tree Gap in various accounts of Civil War skirmishes at the place. His location of Holly Tree Gap was based on the Benton story.

Nashville historian Stanley Horn agrees with Hooberry, basing his view on the Benton account, official Civil War reports, and his belief that the Granny White Pike turned westward through the hills before swinging east to the Franklin Road, coming in south of "Hollow Tree Gap" and thus bypassing it. This last belief is based on topography and the military strategy involved in Hood's retreat after the Battle of Nashville. It would explain the Confederate stand in the gap, designed to keep open the road in their rear for stragglers from the Granny White Pike.

We could not, however, find a single old resident in the vicinity who remembered hearing the Granny White Gap called Holly Tree Gap. Nor could we find any historical or literary reference to it as such, including Civil War accounts, except the Benton reference already quoted.

In 1849-50 the State Legislature, in granting a turnpike charter, called it "White's Gap," but in 1852 William Wales, reporting for the *Southwestern Monthly,* wrote that he passed through the "Holly Tree Gap . . . ten miles or thereabouts" south of the city.

The Franklin Road gap is spelled "Holly" and "Hollow" on the same page (532) of *Hancock's Diary,* a Civil War journal, lending credence to Park Marshal's remark that "these (meaning soldiers) are not good witnesses."

In Williamson County, court records the name of the gap on Franklin Road is spelled both ways, but Marshall wrote that "the best men in the county, time out of mind" had said the correct spelling was "Holly" and that an evergreen tree stood at the spot.

The Wales reference mentioned Barton's Fort, four miles north of "Holly Tree Gap" and other hints that may eventually solve the riddle.

History and blue-green hills compete for attention out the Granny White Pike. Beginning on Twelfth Avenue, just beyond where Acklen crosses, here are some of the sights.

The hill, rising to the right at Bate Avenue, marked a strong point in the federal defense line around occupied Nashville during the Civil War. The old WSM-TV tower stands atop the hill.

Dallas Avenue comes in from the right in the Waverly area. Here Mrs. Bettie Fudge, a great-granddaughter of Granny White, died in 1935 at the age of ninety-two. She died at the home of her niece, Mrs. Walter Gray, not far from the location of the first tollgate on the pike. She was the daughter of Mr. and Mrs. John Sawyers.

On the left, at Kirkwood Lane, stands the old Granville Sevier mansion in the center of Sevier Park. Built by the Adams family, this old home was once owned by Mrs. Jesse Benton. At various times it was called Idlewild and Lee-Monte.

Tradition has it that the old log cabins behind this house were built by French fur traders in the years before Englishmen came over the mountains. The claim is a respectable one, and if it is true, they are the oldest buildings in this part of the country.

Cedar Lane goes off to the right, up to the hill where the Montgomery mansion once stood, and one of its "dependencies" still stands. Here Hood's skirmish line met the first shock of the federal attack on December 15, 1864.

Where Shackleford Road comes in from the right, the land rises sharply to Vinegar Hill. On a farm called Vinegar Hill,

four miles from Nashville on the Granny White Pike, lived
Colonel Frank McNairy, Confederate hero who was killed at
the second battle of Fort Donelson.

At Draughon Avenue stands the ante-bellum home of Mrs.
W. T. Berry, widow of the direct descendant of the early Nash-
ville bookseller, W. T. Berry. Beautifully bound volumes from
Berry's personal collection are kept in her home.

On Duncanwood Drive stood the Johns house, a landmark
of the Battle of Nashville. The home of Mrs. Whitten Duncan
is built on the old foundations.

On Lipscomb Drive the white frame home of C. C. Franck
is built on the foundations of the old Bradford home. Here Miss
Mary Bradford ran into the road, "under heavy fire," and
pleaded with the veterans of Deas' Confederate Brigade to halt
their retreat. She begged the men to rally and fight, but the
beaten soldiers ignored her tears and continued to the rear.

To the right of Harding Place-Battery Lane rises Shy's Hill,
where Hood's line was broken on the second day and the gallant
Colonel William Shy was killed.

At Sewanee Road, to the left, at the home of E. A. Bergstrom,
begins the stone wall which formed the northern boundary of
Lealand, the home of Judge John M. Lea. Loring's division of
Stewart's Corps was posted behind this wall on the second day
of battle.

In the gap is a reproduction, built by Mr. and Mrs. Everett
Beasley, of the old Granny White tavern. Granny White is buried
nearby, her grave marked by a stone and an iron fence.

At the corner of Otter Creek Road and Granny White Pike
stands a country store operated by W. E. Whitmore. It is comparatively modern, but not many such stores are left.

Farther along on the left is a blacksmith shop, operated until
about 1957 by Ed Jennette, who lived there. It is now abandoned.

The tollgate house, built of logs, stands abandoned by the
road, on the left, just north of Old Hickory Boulevard. Old
residents say there were no tollgates on the pike, but the records
say there were, as did the obituary of Mrs. Fudge. Neighbors
say this house was never used for that purpose.

The Johnson Chapel Methodist Church has an old cemetery

that goes back to earliest days. A Confederate soldier, who fought within a few hundred yards of the place, wrote that "my grandfather was buried there." Near this church a part of Forrest's Cavalry stood off the Federals for the night in the pitch darkness of Hood's retreat toward the Franklin Road. Here Colonel Ed Rucker of the Twelfth Tennessee Confederate Cavalry fought a saber duel with Colonel George Spalding of the Twelfth Tennessee Federal Cavalry. Rucker was captured when a pistol shot broke his arm.

Beyond the old Brentwood Road, which crosses near the church, according to tradition the pike passed through the canebrakes and hills, and continued "by a woodland way" to Franklin.

SICK INDIAN AND GOLD BRICK

Daylight faded and December dusk closed in on downtown Nashville. Snowflakes swirled around gas lamps that made pools of light on the streets. Salesmen and shoppers crowded into horse-drawn streetcars as the evening rush hour began.

In his office on Church Street, financier Allen F. Leonte could take a comfortable view of the scene beneath his window. Leonte (that's not his real name) was a founder of the Merchants' Exchange. His milling and grocery businesses were prosperous. His name on a slip of paper was good for any sum in Nashville's market place. While Leonte read market reports and waited for his carriage, some downtowners, deciding to tarry a while, dropped in at the Climax Saloon and Gambling House. (The building was across the street from the Maxwell House.)

Inside the Climax the soft rattle of dice and occasional popping of corks were subdued by the tinkle of "The Kiss Waltz" on the house piano. Some of the visitors noticed that Spot Mc-Carthy was missing from this cheery haunt—his usual hangout. Other gamblers shook the dice cup and dealt aces and jacks. Spot was not to be found.

At Shelby Bottom, on that long ago evening in 1880, there were no gaslights there to catch the falling snowflakes. Across the low, vacant land near the river walked a lonely Indian. Bearing a heavy burden, he walked slower and slower through the deepening snow, then he halted. The Indian chief—for he would be remembered as Chief Hennessee of an unknown tribe—opened his pack. And soon a lonely tepee stood beside

139

the Cumberland. The chief drew warm blankets around him and lay down to sleep.

Before darkness had closed in, another figure appeared in the bottom. Bob Boston stuck his head in the tent flap.

"Hey, Spot," he called softly, "have you got it?"

The Indian, who was none other than Spot McCarthy, went into his act.

"Me sick," said the chief in muffled tones from under his blanket.

"Heap sick Indian, eh?" said Bob. "What's that you've got there shining under the blanket?"

"Me gottum gold brick."

Bob Boston laughed. "All right, Spot," he said. "Hope you've got something to keep you warm. I'll see you tomorrow."

And so the conference ended.

The next morning, in his office on Church Street, Allen Leonte heard the story from Bob Boston. An Indian chief, it appeared, had been making his way from a western reservation to Washington. The purpose of his trip was to take a gold brick to the nation's capital, where he expected to have it made into golden coin of the realm.

But it developed, Bob continued, that the Indian had fallen sick in Nashville, and was even then encamped in the Shelby Bottom beside the river. The chief needed money, and would sell his gold brick for five thousand dollars. There was opportunity here, said Bob, because he figured the brick was worth ten thousand dollars or maybe more.

Leonte heard the story through, gave Boston a hard look, and laughed. "This is the oldest skin game in the country," he said. "It's ridiculous. Do I look like the kind of man who'd buy a gold brick?"

Boston stood his ground. "All right," he said, "if that's the way you feel about it. But let me tell you one thing. I think that brick is pure gold."

Leonte thought a moment. "Well," he said, "there are ways to find out. We'll go down to the bottom this afternoon and see the chief's brick."

The ailing Chief Hennessee seemed barely able to grunt, but

he admitted he had a gold brick and would part with it for five thousand dollars. Cautiously he pulled back his blanket and exposed a tiny corner of the great nugget. With his pen knife, Leonte scraped a few flakes of metal from the surface. It looked like gold.

Back to town the financier went, and early next morning he had his answer from an expert jeweler at Stief's. The metal was pure gold.

As a business proposition, it looked like a good thing. The chief was willing to sell and ride the railroad train back to his reservation. There would be a handsome profit in it for Leonte. So back to the lonely tepee Leonte went, and soon he was the owner of the gold brick—a nugget so heavy it burdened a man to carry it. And Chief Hennessee had his money.

What happened next is predictable.

Leonte took his brick to the bank. The skeptical banker tested it and found it pure lead—except for a tiny amount of gold that had come up on Leonte's knife blade. The oldest confidence game in the country had worked again. Leonte stormed back out to Shelby Bottom, but the tepee was gone—and so was the sick Indian chief.

That night Spot McCarthy, in a high starched collar, was dealing the cards again at the Climax. He was very much in the chips.

Another version of the story has it that the brick was sold by a real Indian, held in the custody of blue-uniformed U.S. cavalrymen who were taking him to a federal prison in Florida. The cavalrymen, according to this account, were play-acting Nashvillians who, having sold the brick to Leonte as a practical joke, gave the five thousand dollars to charity. But this version is not so widely told—or as widely believed—as the story of Spot McCarthy in the role of Chief Hennessee.

Whatever the case, Leonte was chagrined, to put it mildly. He had been fooled, and as one man said, in those days not many people fooled Allen Leonte. He didn't like to talk about the deal, and he didn't prosecute anybody. Nor did he try to catch the chief. And the story could end there, but it didn't.

Leonte found out who the chief really was. Perhaps he saw

him occasionally around the Maxwell House. As the years went by, Spot McCarthy didn't fare well. He lost his touch with the dice. He was crippled and walked with a cane, a familiar and somewhat pitiful sight on the sidewalks of downtown Nashville.

And then one morning, Spot was dead. His widow grieved, and at his usual haunts old cronies were sad. So Spot was laid to rest, with suitable ceremonies.

A few days later his widow, who was left penniless, received in the mail a check for a large sum of money. The man who signed the check was the man who bought Spot McCarthy's gold brick—Allen Leonte.

CENTENNIAL JEWEL

The most beautiful and best loved of all Nashville's treasures is the Parthenon. On summer nights the great building stands in a sea of green grass, glowing jewel-like under yellow lights. On wintry days it catches color and life from pale sunlight, reflecting the "glory of Greece" by the shore of Lake Watauga, in Centennial Park.

The original Parthenon was built on the Acropolis, 200 feet above the streets of Athens, 438 years before Christ was born. The building was a shrine honoring Athena Parthenos, Greek goddess of beauty and wisdom.

The builder of the beautiful temple on the hill was Phidias, the "greatest artist of form" the world has ever known. For more than a thousand years the Greeks worshiped Athena in her temple, and the ruin of the Parthenon stands in Athens today. Had it not been for a gunpowder explosion in 1787 it would be as beautiful as it ever was.

The man responsible for Nashville's Parthenon was a "little giant," an energetic, bearded man who was both artist and engineer, Major Eugene C. Lewis. As director general of the Tennessee Centennial Exposition, Lewis conceived his idea for the Parthenon in 1895, planning the Athenian temple as the cultural and architectural showpiece of the great exposition in 1897.

The moving spirit in building the park, as in building the Parthenon, was again the "Little Giant," E. C. Lewis. And in the summer of 1913 all of Nashville paid tribute to him.

Built to last a year, the "Centennial" Parthenon stood twenty-four years, but by 1920 it was falling down. Then Nashville's board of park commissioners set itself to a mighty task— the building of a new and permanent Parthenon. They tore the old building down and went to work.

The architects were Hart, Freeland, and Roberts. The sculptors were Belle Kinney, Leopold Scholz, and George J. Zolnay. Time, effort, and money were not spared to build an accurate reproduction of the original Greek temple, both from architectural and artistic points of view. On May 20, 1931, after eleven years of labor, the building was opened to the public.

The architecture of the Parthenon is Doric, although there are four Ionic columns in the West Room, or Maidens' Chamber. The most striking feature of the interior is the Naos, or temple proper, surrounded by a double row of Doric columns. Casts of the Elgin Marbles are displayed in this room.

The east pediment contains thirty-one sculptures of Greek gods and goddesses and tells the story of the birth of Athena, springing full-grown and clothed in armor, from the head of Zeus.

Sculptures on the west pediment portray the great struggle between Poseidon, god of the sea, and his niece Athena for the land of ancient Greece. Athena's gift of the olive tree was counted greater than Poseidon's gift of the sea, and she was the victor.

There are historic reminders of Centennial Exposition days in the park and some of a much earlier time. Near the West End fence stands a great oak tree which marks the site, on the Natchez Trace, of a blacksmith shop operated by John Cockrill, a pioneer settler who married a sister of James Robertson and was the grandfather of Mark Cockrill, Tennessee's most famous farmer.

Across the road from the spring, which flows in a sewer beneath iron gratings, is the little shell spring for which Major Lewis cast the concrete shell-roof for the exposition—and with proper planting and care it would still be beautiful. It is said that the major went to the Florida coast, found a sea shell he liked, and copied it exactly for this unusual little spring house.

TALLEST OF THE TRIO

Nighttime travelers in the hills around Nashville cannot fail to see and admire the golden necklace of lights atop the city reservoir. That circle of yellow sparklers marks the Federal "strong point" of Civil War days on Franklin Pike. The great four-lane highway that was once a buffalo path to the salt lick on the Cumberland, passes through a saddle in the first chain of hills that circles the city from the river above to the river below. And it was three of these hills that caught the eye of the Federal Army engineer whose duty it was to fortify occupied Nashville back in 1863.

To the right of the pike coming into the city, stood St. Cloud Hill, lowest of the three, rising 258 feet above low-water mark on the Cumberland. There was a fine stand of oak trees on its slopes in the happy, bustling days between the Indian War and the "late unpleasantness." The wooded hill was a favorite spot for picnickers on Sunday afternoons. But the war came, and John Trotwood Moore was to write: "Out from Negley's frowning brow . . ." It is doubtful if anybody has picnicked there since.

Just left of the road rose Kirkpatrick's hill, tallest of the trio, standing 316 feet above low water. On its crest the city reservoir stands today. And 300 yards northward was Currey's Hill, sometimes called Meridian Hill and more recently Rock Crusher Hill, 291 feet high.

It was a man from Philadelphia, James St. Clair Morton, who was to change the name of all the hills, for a time. He fortified them with embrasures and cannon, and on their crests

he stationed men in blue uniforms. They thus became the tri-
ple-threat strong point of the Federal defense line around Nashville.

Kirkpatrick's Hill became Fort Casino, and just behind it
Currey's Hill supported Fort Morton, named for its builder, its
guns supporting Casino. Across Franklin Road Fort Negley was
built on St. Cloud. This bristling redoubt was restored by the
Works Progress Administration during the Great Depression
of the late thirties. It has not been maintained by the city,
however, and today its crest is pretty well grown up in weeds
and scrub timber.

General James S. Negley, for whom the fort was named, had
an excellent record in the Union army until the battle of Chickamauga, where his retreat was considered too precipitate by
his superiors.

On Kirkpatrick's Hill stands that great stone structure, the
city reservoir, which has stood, in a manner of speaking, since
1889. On top of the reservoir stands a quaint little red cottage
which seems to be suited to be the "abode of the good spirit
of the water works." This idea is not far from the truth since
the small structure houses the valves which control the water
supply in that area.

From the rim of the great tank, which may be visited by
special permission only, one can take a 360 degree tour of the
city of Nashville with a fine view of the downtown section, the
university area, and the hills and ridges around the city.

It is a third of a mile around the rim of the reservoir, which
holds fifty million gallons and is usually almost full. The water,
which is pumped four miles from the pumping station on the
Cumberland, is stored in two sections of twenty-five million
gallons each, one being used while the other is being treated.
The stone walls of the reservoir are thirty-three feet high, thirty
feet thick at the base and ten feet thick at the top. They look
strong but . . .

It was a few minutes after midnight on election day, November
5, 1912, when the southeast stone wall of the reservoir gave
way.

A wall of water five feet high came roaring down the hill,

with great stones from the broken wall riding on its crest. A number of houses were washed off their foundations by twenty-five million gallons of good drinking water (only half the reservoir was affected). Streets were blocked by stones and debris, but by great good luck nobody was drowned or even seriously injured.

Citizens of Waverly Place and streets near the reservoir, however, didn't appreciate their icy midnight bath, and they strove mightily but in vain to prevent the city from repairing the reservoir on that site.

Olympic Street runs from Twelfth Avenue to the site of Fort Morton on Currey's Hill, but now you wouldn't call that hill Olympus, by any stretch of the imagination.

The top of the hill is gone, removed by men and machines when the city quarried rock from the site over a period of many years. (The great pit of the rock quarry was later filled. Today it is the site of Rose Park.)

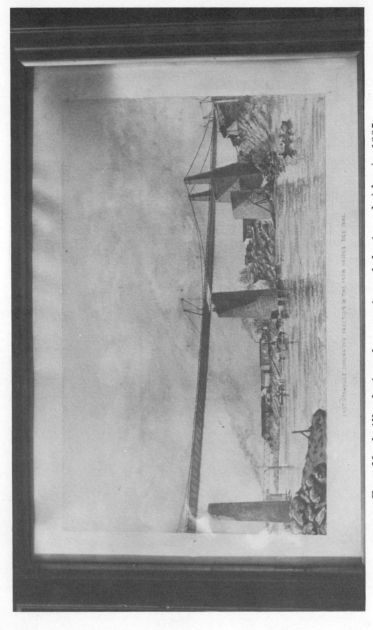

East Nashville during the erection of the iron bridge in 1885.

BRIDGES OF NASHVILLE

The Cumberland River, running west and a little north from Carthage, dips southward in a long, shallow bend to Nashville, splitting the city in two. From earliest times the river provided a valuable means of transportation and at the same time a barrier to transportation—depending on which way you wanted to go.

The first settlers, coming down from the northeast in 1779, crossed the Cumberland on a natural bridge of ice—but the times when Mother Nature provided such a toll-free crossing have been few and far between.

From the beginning there were stations on both sides of the river, and ferry boats did a profitable business. By 1820 Nashville had a population of three thousand, steamboats were arriving at the foot of Broad Street, and the citizens decided to bridge the Cumberland.

Despite the financial panic of 1819-1820, bridge and steamboat companies were organized at about the same time, with sales of stock a little slow. Robert Weakley was president of the bridge company and R. Farquharson, secretary.

The first bridge was built from the northeast corner of the square to the Gallatin turnpike, where the Victory Memorial Bridge now stands. Early writers like to refer to it as "the substantial and elegant" bridge across the Cumberland.

Nashville's first bridge was widely known as the "Stone Bridge," but only the piers were of stone. Built by Stacker & Johnston of Pittsburgh, it contained twenty thousand feet of lumber and twenty-six tons of iron, and cost eighty-five thousand dollars. It was a three-arch bridge, 560 feet long and 40 feet wide, built 75 feet above low water mark.

On May 11, 1821, the first Catholic mass was held in Nashville, and most of the sixty Catholics present were workmen who had come from Pittsburgh, Cincinnati, and Louisville to work on the new bridge.

On November 14, 1851, when workmen were dismantling the old bridge, it collapsed and fell into the river. The accident occurred just after the men had stopped work for the day.

"Beautiful" is the adjective generally used to describe Nashville's second bridge, a suspension span which hung over the river from stone piers on either bank, crossing where the Woodland Street Bridge is now. The first wire was stretched across on May 22, 1850, and on June 28, the first horse and buggy crossed over.

The architect for the suspension bridge was Adolphus Heiman of Nashville, who later commanded the Tenth Tennessee Regiment at Fort Donelson. The contractor was Captain M. D. Fields, brother of Cyrus Fields, who laid the first Atlantic cable. It was 700 feet long, and 110 feet above low water.

On the night of February 18, 1862, Confederate soldiers under General John B. Floyd cut the cables of the suspension bridge, wrecking the structure. The same night they burned the railroad bridge, built just before the war by A. Anderson and Wilbur Foster for the Louisville and Nashville and Edgefield and Kentucky Railroads.

This bridge, just below the Victory Memorial Bridge, still serves the L&N Railroad but has been strengthened for heavier loads. Its two draw spans, which could (and still can be) turned aside to admit the passage of tall-stacked steamers, were the longest in the country at the time the bridge was built.

Nashville's fine bridges were destroyed by retreating Confederates "very unwisely" (Crew) and "against the earnest protest of the leading citizens" (Clayton). The Federal army soon repaired the railroad bridge, laying plank beside the rails to permit its use by wagons. For miles up and down the river, on quiet nights, country people could hear the rattling of the boards as Yankee provision wagons crossed the bridge at Nashville.

In 1866, the first year after the war, the suspension bridge was "reconstructed" with Major Wilbur Foster in charge of the work. The new bridge served the city twenty years until it was condemned and taken down.

In 1886 Nashville built the Woodland Street Bridge to replace the last suspension bridge, spanning the river east to what was then called Bridge Avenue. It is safe to say that more people and vehicles crossed this bridge than any other which ever spanned the Cumberland. A mighty structure of iron and stone, it served the city for more than three-quarters of a century.

With four spans resting on three piers, the Woodland Street Bridge was fifty-four feet wide, with two roadways eighteen feet wide and two sidewalks seven feet wide. It was 639 feet long and 93 feet above low water. (The water level is now higher).

On April 10, 1886, the big iron bridge was ready for testing, and some five thousand citizens gathered to watch. Under the command of Captain Pat Cleary of the fire department and Captain G. Bouscaren, an engineer, the following procession marched up on the bridge:

The city's willapus-wallapus, or steam road roller, weighing thirty-two thousand pounds, thirty 2-horse wagons and fourteen carts loaded with broken stone, five fire engines, and a hook and ladder truck. Enough citizens then moved on to bring the total weight on the bridge to well over half a million pounds.

The new bridge took the punishment without a quiver, sagging much less than specifications allowed, but time, rust, and vibration, with ever increasing loads, finally took their toll.

In 1965-1966 the Woodland Street bridge was replaced after eighty-one years of service. A new four-lane span of steel and concrete was dedicated by Mayor Beverly Briley and opened to traffic on December 1, 1966.

The new bridge was built at a cost of $2.2 million. It is supported by two piers, whereas the old bridge had required three, offering some obstruction to traffic on the river.

In the years between the Spanish-American War and the First World War, Nashville built two bridges, the Jefferson Street

Bridge in 1907 and the Sparkman Street (or Shelby) Bridge in 1908. The two bridges are of similar "through truss" design with concrete piers.

On the first of these a construction superintendent amazed his audience—and some workers, too—when he shortened an overlong steel beam by packing it in ice. Sure enough it "drew up," and fell into place.

The fine Victory Memorial Bridge, built by the state of Tennessee where the city's first "Stone Bridge" stood, was completed and opened on July 2, 1956, at a cost of three and a half million dollars. This is a plate girder bridge, with the iron truss gone.

The Silliman Evans Memorial Bridge, built by the state at a cost of seven million, was named for the late publisher of *The Nashville Tennessean* by a resolution of the 1961 General Assembly. The bridge was officially opened on January 14, 1964, when Mrs. Silliman Evans cut the ribbon at the entrance. Highway Commissioner David Pack described this beautiful new span as "the heart of the expressway network in Nashville and—because it is the state capital—the heart of the entire interstate network in Tennessee."

There are more bridges across the Cumberland at Nashville— the new bridge near Madison, in Pennington Bend, the Hyde's Ferry highway bridge at Bordeaux, the Tennessee Central railroad bridge just below it, and the L&N "freight cutoff" bridge that crosses at Shelby Park.

The letters L&N on this last bridge, old residents say, actually stand for "Lewisburg and Northern," which was the name of the freight cutoff when it was built from Brentwood to east Nashville.

Nashville's bridges have known their share of excitement and tragedy. According to family records, Andrew Kane, a young stonemason, fell off the first bridge during its construction in 1822 and was killed.

Several citizens have committed suicide by jumping from the bridges into the river. A generation ago a prominent businessman, having leaped from the Woodland Street span, changed his mind when he struck the cold water of the Cumberland. He called for help and was saved.

In 1958 Raul Garcia, a Mexican high diver traveling with the Tennessee State Fair, dived from the Victory Memorial Bridge and was picked up by a waiting boat.

Nashville has been bridge building for 140 years and is still building.

HISTORIC SUMNER

No Tennessee county is more beautiful than Sumner and none more conscious of an eventful past.

There are three pleasant routes to the heart of the county. Crossing Mansker's Creek on Gallatin Road one passes the site of a fort built in 1780 by long hunter Kasper Mansker, a courageous Dutchman who was one of the earliest settlers in Middle Tennessee and a signer of the Cumberland Compact.

Two miles beyond Mansker's lies the bustling, growing, lakeside town of Hendersonville. Just beyond, on the left, stands the Hendersonville Presbyterian Church, an architectural gem built in 1869, with a churchyard cemetery beside it. The town was named for Richard Henderson, one of the founders of Nashville.

Near Hendersonville, Drake's Creek intersects the highway beside the Berry estate, home of the late Colonel Harry S. Berry and his sister, Miss Sarah Berry. This farm is one of the few Revolutionary land grants still occupied by descendants of the original owner. The grant was made to General Daniel Smith, a surveyor and official of the territory south of the Ohio River before Tennessee became a state.

General Smith's great stone house, Rock Castle, stands well-preserved on an arm of land extending into Old Hickory Lake. Built in Indian days, between 1784 and 1791, the house is one of the oldest in the state.

Beyond the Blue Grass Country Club lies Saundersville, famous for the murder of a Methodist preacher named Isaac

Lindsay about 1830. The murderer, Willis Carroll, was traced to Indian territory by William Saunders, brought home to face trial and hanged for his crime.

A few generations ago Saundersville was called a "flourishing village" by Killebrew in his *Resources of Tennessee*. Hendersonville took second place as "also a thriving village," but time has reversed this verdict. Hendersonville is both thriving and flourishing, but one has to look hard to find Saundersville.

Near Saundersville a country road entering from the north leads to the site of an ancient Indian village, once inhabited by prehistoric Stone Grave people. The village is mapped and described in Thruston's *Antiquities of Tennessee*. Some years ago the great mound was plainly visible, with arrowheads and stone-skinning knives still to be found in the area. The village site is on the old Rutherford-Kizer farms, later owned by Lawson and Camper.

The country near Gallatin is famous for its bluegrass—and the blue water of Old Hickory Lake. Near the town the highway passes the site of the once popular Grassland Downs steeplechase. Here, during the twenties, sportsmen from many states watched the annual race for the King of Spain cup. The colorful event folded during the depression years.

South and east of Gallatin, on a sweeping bend of the Cumberland, lies the ancient "port" of Cairo, pronounced "Kayro." It has sometimes been confused with "Ca Ira," a town planned in the area by the Tennessee legislature but never built. Once an important landing for river boats, Cairo had tobacco and cotton warehouses long before the Civil War, along with a silversmith's shop and a general store. The community is described in detail in Eastin Morris' *Tennessee Gazeteer*. As the newer town of Gallatin grew, old Cairo declined, and not until the opening of Old Hickory Lake did the abandoned village stir from its slumbers.

Cairo was named for Cairo, Egypt, by the operator of its largest store, General James Winchester. His great stone house, Cragfont, is now a museum house near Castalian Springs. One old store building, a reminder of better days, is still standing.

Less than two miles north of Cairo, on a farm owned by John

Bell Brimm, lie chimney stones marking the site of Ziegler's
station, where Jacob Ziegler and Archie Wilson were killed by
Indians on the night of June 26, 1792. Women and children
were captured by the Cherokee marauders and taken to the
Indian towns on the Tennessee River. Some escaped later or
were ransomed. The spring house, built of stone by Jacob Ziegler,
is still intact. Brimm knows the exact spot where Ziegler lost
his life. Standing beside the stone reminders of a forgotten
tragedy, one can look across the little valley where Elizabeth
Ziegler fled through a canebrake on that terrible night, smother-
ing the cries of her children, stumbling and running until she
reached neighbors and safety in Cairo.

Sunken roads, log houses, and giant trees in the fence rows
tell a story of antiquity in Sumner County, and nowhere are
these more in evidence than at Castalian Springs, which in early
days was called Bledsoe's Lick.

Highway 25 does not quite touch Castalian Springs but passes
just to the north of it, dividing the beautiful Wynnewood farm.
The most attractive building of the village is the log home of
Mr. and Mrs. George Wynne, unchanged since it was built in
1828. The great log house, set on the side of a wooded hill,
stands in a historic region of rare beauty. George Wynne is a
descendant of General James Winchester, and his family has
lived in the valley of Bledsoe's Lick Creek since pioneer days.
Across the stream is a green-capped mound made by prehistoric
Indians, first excavated by Ralph E. W. Earl in 1821.

Portrait painter and friend of Andrew Jackson, Earl was also
manager of the Nashville museum. His detailed report on the
excavation appeared in 1823 in Haywood's *Natural and Aboriginal History of Tennessee*. A century later further excava-
tions were made by the Carthage archeologist, W. E. Myer, and
sandstone images were found.

Although the place has been called Castalian Springs for more
than a century, George Wynne prefers the more historic but
less romantic name of Bledsoe's Lick. The place was discovered
by long hunter and early settler Isaac Bledsoe, who first saw
it before a permanent white settlement had been made on the
Cumberland.

In pioneer days every salt spring was called a lick. Here, buffalo, deer, and bear found water and minerals and here, too, came the Indian, the long hunter, and the first settlers.

When Bledsoe first saw the land around the lick it was covered by a herd of buffalo. He shot one, but so great was the crush and the stampede that he was unable to get off his horse, and the dead buffalo was trampled into the earth.

Some time later Bledsoe returned to the lick and hardly recognized it—the hunters had been at work. White bones of the buffalo were scattered thick around the spring. Hunters had taken only choice cuts of meat, and grass around the area grew tall, fertilized by the bodies of slain animals.

On a hill beside the lick, the Bledsoe brothers, Isaac and Anthony, lie buried in a small graveyard, both slain by Indians. In 1907 a monument was erected to the brothers in the little cemetery by J. G. Cisco and members of the Bledsoe family. Two hundred yards west of the cemetery is the site of Bledsoe's Station, on the Charles Belote farm, where the earliest residents of the county found shelter and a measure of safety from hostile Indians. Cragfont, Hall's Station, and the site of Spencer's tree are other landmarks of Castalian Springs. Two miles to the north, on rising ground beside an ancient spring, is the little-known site of Greenfield Station, the fort built by Anthony Bledsoe, scene of one of the most colorful Indian battles in Tennessee history. The old home of Nathaniel Parker, who married Bledsoe's widow, stands nearby. The farm where the house stands has long been known as the Russel Wilson farm but is now owned by Dr. Thomas Parrish. Its long driveway is entered from the Rock Spring Road, which takes its name from Bledsoe's Spring.

The rock wall Anthony Bledsoe built around his spring is still there, though some of the stones are tumbling down, and the cool spring is clear as crystal. The rock fence, off which one Indian was shot, still borders the field called "Old Troublesome," where the battle began.

Greenfield is close to the "ridge," a line of hills to the north which marks the beginning of the Highland Rim. In these hills rise the creeks—Drake's, Station Camp, and Bledsoe's, which flow through the rich bottomland and empty into the Cumberland.

Another historic trip from Nashville to Gallatin is by way of the Long Hollow Road from Goodlettsville. The town is named for Dr. Adam B. Goodlet, who married Eliza Turner and "set up housekeeping" there in 1834. The long Hollow Road is well-named for the countryside through which it meanders. The "long hollow" between high ridges extends for miles along Madison Creek. The creek bed is worn deep through solid rock, the stone fences are mossy and tumble-down, and trees along the fence rows are tall and well-grown.

Two miles from Goodlettsville, just beyond the Madison Baptist Church, stands the old farm owned by Gilbert Shreeve, boasting "gingerbread" trim and colorful stained-glass windows. In this old house two bullet holes, twenty-five feet apart, tell a grim story of the dark days of 1864. Bushwhackers, bent on robbery, fired through a one-inch wooden door to kill Darby Cantrell, builder of the house, as he stood on the stair. Cantrell's fifteen-year-old son fired an answering shot that missed, and his bullet is still embedded in the wall.

Five miles up the road at Shackle Island stands the Old Beech Cumberland Presbyterian Church, organized in 1789 with the present building constructed thirty years later. The cemetery in the churchyard is one of the oldest in the county, and it is believed that the "western-most" soldier of the Revolution is buried here.

Shackle Island lies on Drake's Creek just beyond the Beech Church. According to some old residents, the place was named for a tavern keeper named Shackle, who ran his establishment between the creek and a nearby branch on what was called "the island." The community was founded by William Montgomery, who built two of the three fine old homes still standing in the area, the first in 1812.

Crossing Station Camp Creek, along which stood many early blockhouses, the traveler reaches the site of the old John Hamilton house, scene of the first meeting of the county court of Sumner County. The site is marked by the Colonel Jethro Sumner chapter of the DAR.

As the traveler reaches Two Mile Creek, he is on the outskirts of Gallatin. Here he may, if he wishes, swing left toward Springfield and the Red River country.

A third route from Nashville to Gallatin is by way of Lebanon Road to the vicinity of Martha, once a station on the Tennessee Central Railroad. Here a road to the north passes through beautiful fields to the Woods Ferry Bridge across the Cumberland, one of the prettiest bridges on the river. North of the bridge is the Guild house on the outskirts of Gallatin, scene of a dramatic incident of the Civil War. Confederate soldier George Guild "stole home" to see his family. He found the house surrounded by Yankees, but managed to get in and spend the night.

The old home, called Rosemont, built by Judge Josephus Conn Guild, is crumbling under the assaults of time and weather. It was here that Judge Guild wrote his classic book of reminiscences, *Old Times in Tennessee.*

THE RAW IRISHMAN

They never molded the bullet that could kill Hugh Rogan. He was destined to die in bed, in a green valley of Sumner County.

However, Creek Indians did have bullets that would puncture the hide of the Irish pioneer, and they used them to good effect. Hot-blooded and warm-hearted, Rogan fought them year in and year out, and gave as good as he got.

Rogan's life story—and love story—were epics of Tennessee history, told to sleepy children in the nighttime stillness of frontier log cabins. Rogan was the kind of man who could walk home from an Indian fight with his rifle on his shoulder and a bullet hole in his lung; or run through the night with a coal of fire, with Indians all about, to gratify a dying man's last wish, or go back to the Old Country for his Irish lassie, after twenty years, to bring her to Sumner County.

The story of Rogan's life has never been told before. But brief references in county histories, old letters in the Draper manuscripts, family records, and traditions reveal the colorful career of a man who was called "a raw Irishman."

Hugh Rogan came to the Cumberland County with John Donelson in the spring of 1780, down the Tennessee and up the Cumberland to the site of Nashville. Rocks, rapids, red Indians, and smallpox menaced the little party, but April found them on the Bluffs at Nashville. Rogan moved out with Donelson to a camp at Clover Bottom, then called Old Fields, in

161

the valley of Stone's River. They made a corn crop that summer, but before they could harvest it, the bloodletting began.

Bands of Creeks and Cherokees fell upon the outlying stations, and murders and ambushes became so frequent that Donelson and his party, including Rogan, abandoned the Clover Bottom camp and moved to Mansker's Station, near the present boundary line between Davidson and Sumner counties, on Mansker's Creek.

John Donelson was determined to harvest his corn. He sent his son, Captain John, and along with him went Hugh Rogan, John Robertson, a son of James Robertson, Abel Gower, Abel Gower, Jr., and William Cartwright. The party rowed up Stone's River to the bottom in little boats, and Hugh Rogan got his first taste of Indian fighting. It was a bitter experience. The ambush was quick and sudden, and the white men were caught in their boats, unprepared. Robertson and the two Gowers were killed, and Donelson and Rogan barely escaped and made their way to Mansker's.

The settlement at Mansker's was now broken up, and one of the settlers, James McCain, reported that all who could get horses went to Kentucky.

"That brave Irishman, Hugh Rogan," wrote historian John Carr, "took charge of the widow Neely and her family, and conducted them in safety to Kentucky. I knew him well, and can say truly, he was a soldier and a patriot."

Historian J. G. Cisco wrote that Rogan was "a man without fear, with a big, kind heart, and was a general favorite among the pioneers. He was one of the signers of the Cumberland Compact."

Rogan did not stay long in Kentucky, but came back to Bledsoe's Fort, where Castalian Springs now is. It was here on the night of July 20, 1788, that he made himself the hero of many a bedtime story.

Colonel Anthony Bledsoe and a servant named Campbell were lured out of the fort that night by the sound of Indian whoops and the clatter of horses' hooves on the rocky road. The Indians fired and both men were hit by the same bullet. When they were brought into the house it was found that Campbell was dead, and Bledsoe had but a few hours to live. Rogan and two other men in the fort stood by the loopholes, expecting an attack but none came.

Now it developed that the dying Bledsoe wanted to make a will. He had two sons and seven daughters, and, under North Carolina law of that day, only his sons could inherit his land if he died without a will. He wanted to protect the rights of his daughters. There was no fire in the fort that summer night, and such moonlight as filtered through the chinks and loopholes was not enough. There were no matches in those days. People worked by day and slept by night.

Hugh Rogan said that a man ought to have his last wish granted—and it is the only remark he ever made, as far as we know, that was recorded for posterity. He then plunged out the door, into the night. How Rogan got through the Indians, estimated as a party of fifty, we will never know, but he did get through to the home of the widow Shaver, a mile away. Her husband had been killed by Indians years before, and the Creeks and Cherokees, believing she was a witch, now left her alone.

Did Rogan run back through the woods with a burning brand in his hand? If so, perhaps the sight was enough to frighten the superstitious Indians. If he carried a coal of fire in a pot, perhaps the Indians didn't see him at all. At any rate, Rogan brought the light and Anthony Bledsoe wrote his will beginning: "In the name of God. Amen. Being near to death I make my will as follows . . ."

Rogan called his rifle "the Good Queen Anne," and a family tradition is that he once killed an Indian with the butt of the gun. Rogan had an affinity for Indian fights and hardly ever missed one in his vicinity. In 1787 he was a soldier on the Coldwater Expedition led by James Robertson. The purpose of this raid was to wipe out the town of Coldwater on the Tennessee River where Tuscumbia now stands. The place had been built up by lawless bands of Cherokees and Creeks, aided and abetted by half a dozen French traders. The full-time occupation of these Indians was preying upon the lives and property of settlers on the Cumberland.

The overland expedition against Coldwater was successful, and the village was surprised and wiped out. A number of Indians were killed, as were several Frenchmen and one white woman, who got into a boat with the Indians and, according to Haywood, "seemed determined to share their fate." Goods captured at Coldwater were brought to Eaton's Station and sold at auction. Proceeds were divided among the troops.

All of this was, of course, a great success. In the meantime Hugh Rogan, serving in the waterborne section of the expedition, had run into unexpected trouble. David Hay of Nashville commanded this flotilla, which speedily descended the Cumberland, but was so becalmed on the Tennessee that sails were of no use, and poles and oars were laboriously brought into action. At the mouth of Duck River, Captain Moses Shelby, in command of one of the boats, decided to investigate a canoe which was tied to a sapling on the bank. As the boat pulled near the bank it was fired on by a party of Indians, lying hidden in the thick cane. Joseph Renfroe was shot through the head, and Rogan through the body, the bullet piercing one lung. Renfroe died before he left the boat, and the manner of his death caused some head shaking and wonderment.

"It was a singular coincidence," says Clayton's *History of Davidson County*, "that though shot through the brain, he still retained the use of some of his faculties. The crew had been spearing fish with sharpened canes, and as they proceeded on water for some time after the repulse, Renfroe sat upright in the bow of the boat and speared at real or imaginary fish until he died; but it was quite probable the act was a phase of 'unconscious cerebration' in which he repeated the train of ideas that was dominant in his mind up until a few moments of the reception of his injury."

The historian then remarked that Rogan was an Irishman of superlative courage and strength of will and though he was shot through one lung he not only marched home without assistance but "carried his gun and accouterments."

Rogan was in other desperate encounters of which little is known. "In 1782 or 1783," as Carr puts it, he was with General Daniel Smith near where Cragfont now is, on the buffalo trail

between Mansker's and Bledsoe's Licks, when they were attacked by Indians. A man named Memury was killed and General Smith wounded.

In 1787 Rogan was on the scene when the Hall family was
attacked by Indians near the Locust Land, north of Bledsoe's
Lick. What part he played in the fight we do not know. Later,
Governor William Hall wrote:

"My little brother and sister ran back to the house, but with
the alarmed dogs barking at them, they ran back to the scene
of the battle. Here they found Mr. Rogan's hat, which the little
boy picked up."

Hugh Rogan was born in Glentourn, County Donegal, Ireland,
in 1747. He married Ann (Nancy) Duffy and they had one son,
Bernard, born in 1774. Rogan served with the "Irish Defenders"
under Harry Grattan, and when that chief was arrested he
slipped out in 1775, leaving his wife and son in Ireland. Sailing
to America on the last merchant ship to leave before the Revolution, Rogan arrived in Philadelphia a few days after the Battle
of Bunker Hill. He enlisted on the first ship commissioned in
the American Navy, but a Tory trickster intervened.

Rogan had found a job in Philadelphia. His employer was
a Quaker named Downey, a man friendly to the Tories. It was
his responsibility to notify Rogan when to report to his ship.
He did this—a day late, and the ship sailed without the would-be
volunteer.

Rogan moved to North Carolina to a settlement called Hor-
net's Nest, in a "hollow" on the Yadkin River. Here he operated
a store and, according to one account, followed his trade as
a weaver. In 1779 he enlisted as a guard for a company led
by Richard Henderson, Thomas Walker, and Daniel Smith to
survey a line between Virginia and North Carolina. A family
manuscript says Rogan and others of this party remained for
some time on Goose Creek, near where Hartsville now stands,
but by midwinter he was back in East Tennessee in time to
start for the Cumberland country with John Donelson.

Between campaigns, Hugh decided to go back to Ireland for
his wife and son. Such a trip was no easy matter for a poor
soldier to arrange, but because he had planted corn in 1780

he now got a "preemption" of 640 acres of land near where Vanderbilt University now stands. To get money and horses he traded this land for a farm in Sumner County, then set out across country. What happened next is clouded by hazy accounts, but it seems that in North Carolina Rogan ran into a brother-in-law, Daniel Carlin, who had also left a wife in Ireland—and had married again. Carlin knew that if Hugh went back to Ireland he would "tell on him." Carlin concocted and told Rogan a lie. He said Nancy Rogan, thinking her husband dead, had married another man in Ireland. Rogan never doubted the man. Broken-hearted, he came back to Sumner County.

Finally, in 1796, Hugh Rogan's nephew came to Sumner County with a letter from Nancy Rogan in Ireland. It was addressed: "Deliver to your uncle if alive and on the continent of America." In the letter she told Hugh she was still waiting for him. Once again Hugh set out for the Atlantic Coast, and across the sea to Ireland. His baby boy, Bernard, was now a man twenty-two years old. Nancy heard that Hugh Rogan had landed at an Irish port.

"What does he look like?" she asked.

"He is an old man," came the answer, "wearing a tall hat."

"That's not my Hughie," snapped Nancy. "My Hughie is a young man."

But Hugh was her Hughie, and off they went with Bernard to Sumner County, where soon they had another son, Francis. Through him, the couple had nine grandchildren though Hugh, who died in 1813 and is buried on the farm, didn't live to see them.

On his green, rolling Sumner County farm, Hugh Rogan and his Nancy found peace and happiness. The old house still stands today—though how much of it was built by Hugh and how much by his son Francis we do not know. But it is likely that Hugh built the plain stone part, with small windows and straight walls two feet thick—a fortress at the foot of the hills.

The Rogans were Catholics, perhaps the first Irish Catholics in Middle Tennessee and certainly the first in Sumner County, honoring the "Cross and the green." In the practice of their religion they were almost alone in that rural section. Brave and industrious people, they won the respect and affection of their neighbors.

"Rogana," the Rogan farm was called, and when they brought the branch railroad through to Hartsville, the station and village were named for the Irish Indian fighter and farmer, who always came back for another skirmish.

The Rogans are gone from Sumner County now. The village is deserted, the store closed, the post office gone. But descendants of Hugh Rogan, though not numerous, are still to be found in Middle Tennessee, and the tradition of courage he left behind is a permanent part of our Tennessee heritage.

BIG FOOT SPENCER

An elegant historian called him the "Chevalier Beyard of the Cumberland Valley." But most frontiersmen never heard of Beyard, and around their campfires for forty years they told stories of a man they called "Big Foot" Spencer.

In 1775 or 1776, Thomas Sharp Spencer came from Virginia to Bledsoe's Lick in Sumner County, and Dr. E. L. Drake in his *Early Western History* says he was the first settler in Middle Tennessee. He planted corn by 1778 or earlier—the first crop planted by a white man in all the Cumberland country.

"Big Foot" was a big man with a big heart. He was a great hunter and a famous Indian fighter.

"Thomas Spencer was the stoutest man I ever saw," wrote frontier scout and historian John Carr. "Indeed, he was a Hercules—stronger than two ordinary men. Once I rode through a piece of ground cleared by him. There were about five of six acres in the piece. His rail timbers, each of which would have made from ten to fifteen rails, he had cut in the ground, and then had carried them and thrown them around his field.

"One more example of his strength I must not forget. I heard Frank Haney relate that in 1780 Thomas Spencer, Dick Hogan, and himself were raising cabins, that they might obtain titles to the lands settled by them; as at that day all who made improvements obtained 640 acres of land. Hogan was very stout, and bore the name of a bully, and Haney was very little inferior to him in point of strength. They were raising a cabin, while Spencer, being unwell, was in the camp lying on a blanket by the fire. Hogan and Haney had gotten up one end of a log,

169

but for their lives they could not put the other end in place. Spencer, seeing their failure, observed that if he were well he could put the log in place. At this, Hogan became excited, and cursing Spencer, told him he was a better man than he was, any day. Whereupon Spencer, rising, walked to the log, took hold of it, and threw it up with apparent ease, and, without a word, laid down again upon his blanket."

Hogan and Haney, also wordless, went back to their work.

On his frequent visits to Monsieur Demumbrane's store at French Lick (Nashville) Spencer was not a man to be trifled with. Once he took some article from a shelf to examine it and the excitable Frenchman, Drake relates, thinking he meant to take the article by force, struck him in the face. Spencer merely pulled Demumbrane across the counter and greased him from head to foot in a barrel of his own buffalo tallow.

He came off best in several encounters with Indians, and once he saved a neighboring girl from death at their hands.

The incident of the "Broken Knife" illustrates the bigness of Spencer's heart. At Bledsoe's Lick (Castalian Springs) Big Foot spent one winter living in a hollow tree. His companion, a man named Holliday, wanted to return to Virginia, but hesitated to leave, since he had lost his knife and could not skin his meat. Spencer accompanied his friend as far as the "Barrens" of Kentucky. Then he broke his own knife blade into two pieces, gave half to Holliday, and returned to his home in the tree.

Ramsey, in his *Annals of Tennessee,* tells how Big Foot got his nickname:

"Passing one morning the temporary cabin erected at a place since called Eaton's Station (across the river from the French Lick) and occupied by one of Captain Demumbrane's hunters, Spencer's huge tracks were left plainly impressed in the rich alluvial. These were seen by the hunter on his return to camp, who, alarmed at their size, immediately swam across the river, and wandered through the woods until he reached the French settlements on the Wabash."

That part about swimming the river seems a little far fetched—the frightened Frenchman already being on the north side—or perhaps he followed a "circuitous" route to the Wabash!

The creek where Big Foot hunted bear and deer, since called Spencer's Creek, now is a broad embayment of Old Hickory Lake, with a boat dock near its mouth.

"Spencer's Choice" is on the southwest edge of Gallatin. Spencer cleared tracts at Bledsoe's and Greenfield, but when told that he must narrow his choice to one tract, he chose 640 acres of fine land here, ever since known as Spencer's Choice.

Spencer's sister, Elizabeth, who inherited the land, later sold it to David Shelby, who in 1798 built the stone house called Spencer's Choice. It still stands on the edge of advancing subdivisions.

In sharp contrast to the new homes around it, the old stone house with its windowless gables is a silent, sturdy reminder of pioneer days.

At Bledsoe's Lick, Lick Creek flows quietly between the village and the highway—as though protecting the pioneer community from the modern world. Here is the spot where Spencer lived in his hollow tree and planted his crop of corn. To the north he could see the green mound that marks the place where prehistoric Indians lived in the valley, when great herds of buffalo wore a trail through the cane to the salt lick.

In Sumner County Thomas Sharpe Spencer lived in a beautiful valley, fertile and well-watered, but the great Indian fighter met his end on the brow of a high and rugged mountain in what is today Cumberland County—more than a hundred miles from his own fireside.

The big frontiersman had inherited two thousand dollars (a great sum in those days). He was bringing the "yaller gold" back from North Carolina in his saddle bags when the Indians finally caught up with him.

Spencer had a habit of never riding with a large company, always traveling either well-ahead or well-behind, preferring to trust his own powers of observation in detecting an ambush. It was this, says historian E. L. Drake, that finally proved his undoing. Riding ahead of the others, with a man named Walker, he was fired on at close range as he passed under a large rock by the trail. He fell dead on the spot, and Walker was wounded at the same time.

Spencer's horse, rearing and throwing off the gold-filled saddle bags, raced back to the main group. Spencer's horse was soon followed by Walker's. The others turned back on the trail and escaped—but Big Foot, winner of many a wilderness battle, lost his money, his scalp, and his life.

Crab Orchard has become famous for its beautiful "Crab Orchard Stone," a reddish building stone which has been used in many homes and public buildings in Tennessee and elsewhere. The supply seems inexhaustible, and the mining, sizing, and shipping of the stone is a profitable industry in the area.

Just beyond the level plain is Crab Orchard Gap, sometimes called South Pass of the Cumberland Mountains. From here one can see rugged Spencer's Hill, where the road once ran, and where Big Foot was killed. A great shelf of rock, barely visible through the trees, marks the spot of the ambush.

Two Moravian missionaries, Steiner and Schweinitz, who traveled over this road in 1799, kept a journal in which they described the mountain road.

"On the 24th," they wrote, "early in the morning, we crossed the ill-renowned Spencer's Hill. The mountain gets its name from a certain Spencer, one of the first settlers of Cumberland. . . .

"The road is so steep and stony that it seems almost impossible to cross it with a wagon. In the beginning, the road went straight down the mountain and was as steep as a house roof. Now there are roads to the left and to the right down the mountain, but they are all very steep, full of rock slabs, which, often elevated, lie straight across the road.

"A man assured us that he had been obliged to hitch seven horses to an empty wagon in order to draw it up. Wagons cannot go down the mountain otherwise than with a brake on all wheels and with, besides, a great tree hung on behind. On this account the mountain top is already quite denuded with trees."

Many early settlers of Middle Tennessee told their children and grandchildren how they "tied a tree on the wagon" to come down Spencer's hill—and to this day the hill is covered with scrubby pine trees. The great oaks never grew back!

NICKAJACK

It was the late summer of 1794, and to young Charles Bosley the September sun couldn't have shown on a livelier scene than that around Brown's Blockhouse five miles east of Nashville.

Charles was a soldier, just a month shy of his seventeenth birthday, perhaps not much taller than his muzzleloading rifle. And all around him were gathering hundreds of young men like himself, from Middle Tennessee and Kentucky.

The boys, in homespun, didn't look much like an army, but they knew how to ride and shoot, and climb and swim, and they had it in mind to go after bandit Indians—Cherokees and Chickamaugas—across the Tennessee River and wipe them off the earth.

Probably Charles had never seen so many soldiers, for this was the largest army ever assembled in the Cumberland settlement. Hundreds were there and still they kept coming. Colonel William Whitley had brought 150 fighting men from Kentucky—he had come at the personal invitation of Sampson Williams—and Colonel John Montgomery led a sizeable company from around Clarksville in Montgomery County. From all around the settlement at Nashville were men who had answered the call of General James Robertson for volunteers.

Just about this time, as luck or providence would have it, Major James Ore arrived from Knoxville with a company of militia assigned to protect the Cumberland settlements. Ore and his men immediately joined with the frontier army, and to give the expedition the color of legality, Ore officially assumed command.

The real commanders, however, would be such veteran Indian fighters as Colonel Whitley and old Colonel Kasper Mansker, a long hunter and one of the first settlers in the Cumberland country.

Other matters of command were not settled so smoothly. Robert Weakley, who lived three miles east of Nashville, had exerted himself to bring packhorses and provisions to the rendezvous. He then became a candidate for captain but was not elected by the soldiers. Indignant at this lack of appreciation, Robert took his packhorses and provisions and went home.

A. W. Putnam, in his *History of Middle Tennessee,* relates that Weakley afterward became a colonel, a member of the legislature, and "ever a valuable and respected citizen." But the poet Isaac Clark, called the "Homer of the Cumberland," immortalized his retreat from Nickajack in these lines:

> *Colonel Weakley he turned back,*
> *And would not go to Nickajack;*
> *Weakley was his name, and his back—*
> *He could not go to Nickajack;*
> *And his horses with their pack,*
> *Should not go to Nickajack.*
> *Not in courage did he lack,*
> *Though he took the homeward track.*

Besides Whitley and Mansker the gathering army included such veteran Indian fighters as Captain John Rains, a mighty bear hunter, and Edmund Jennings. One of the guides was the famous (or infamous) half-breed, Richard Findleston. This man had warned the settlers two years before of the attack on Buchanan's Station—but he was still not trusted.

The people of the Cumberland settlements had organized the expedition to Nickajack and the Lower Towns of the Chickamaugas on the Tennessee because they were being bled to death by Indians from these villages. Major George Winchester had been shot and killed that summer on the main street of Gallatin while riding to attend court, and Colonel Chew and fifteen men had been ambushed and killed in a boat on the lower Cumberland.

The final outrage was the butchery of two young boys near Rock Castle in Sumner at the home of General Daniel Smith. The two boys, cousins, were both named Anthony Bledsoe.

James Robertson and his Cumberland neighbors could stand no more. Their blood was up, and the September moon had a tinge of reddish gold. No matter what Territorial Governor William Blount had to say in Knoxville, or what the federal government did in Washington, they were going after the Indians.

There was no more determined or braver man in the army than Joe Brown, just a year older than Charles Bosley. Six years before, Indians at Nickajack had boarded his father's boat, pretending friendship. They slipped behind his father and cut off his head with a sword, then murdered Joe Brown's two brothers.

Young Joe was taken prisoner by the Indians, and lived with them in the Lower Towns. One squaw screamed that he should die. "Some day," she cried, "he will guide an army here and destroy our people."

Now young Joe Brown, despite a bullet wound in his shoulder from an Indian ambush, was doing just that. He had scouted the trail in advance, and knew the road well. He had a score to settle at Nickajack.

Nickajack had an evil sound, and even today the cave has an ominous look. Near the point where Tennessee, Alabama, and Georgia come together, a great black hole in the side of the mountain, it looks down on railroad and river, a sullen stream issuing from its mouth. In front of the cave, on a level field near the river, stood the little Indian town of Nickajack, inhabited by Chickamaugas.

Nickajack had gotten its name under bloody circumstances. In 1780 Indian raiders fell upon the men of the Donelson and Gower families as they gathered corn in Clover Bottom on Stone's River. A free Negro man named Jack Civil was slightly wounded and taken prisoner by the Indians. In later years he moved down the Tennessee with the Chickamaugas and lived

Nickajack Cave near Chattanooga.

for a time in the great cave. Over the years Negro Jack became Nickajack, and so the cave got its name.

The army got its orders from Brigadier General James Robertson, who did not go on the expedition. "Destroy the Lower Cherokee towns," wrote Robertson, "taking care to spare the women and children."

On September 9 William Blount, governor of the territory, wrote James Robertson from Knoxville strongly disapproving of the expedition. But he was too late. On Sunday, September 7, the army of 550 horsemen set out on the old Indian warpath. On the first night out, the men camped at the famous Fox Camp Spring, which still flows near Murfreesboro.

On September 12, as darkness fell, the horsemen came to the Tennessee, three miles below the mouth of Sequatchie River. It was dark, and the river was more than half a mile wide. The men tied their horses, and George Flynn was the first to swim across. Being wet and tired, he built a small fire to dry his clothes, whereupon Lieutenant George Blackmore of the Sumner Volunteers, swimming across behind him, "swore and railed so loudly to put out the fire that he committed the worst offense of the two."

The Indians, believing themselves secure in their villages between mountain and river, neither heard the swearing nor saw the fire, and the men kept swimming across, pushing little rafts and boats of cane, wood, and cowhide to transport guns and ammunition. Edmund Jennings, swam the river several times during the night. Major Joseph B. Porter "could not swim one rod, so he got together a bunch of cane, and holding on to it, kicked himself across."

When daylight came it was found that 268 men, about half the army, had gotten across, and they were determined to walk the five miles to Nickajack and attack at once, without waiting for the others, for fear of being discovered by the Indians.

A squad was left to guard two silent Indian houses on the western border of Nickajack Town while the other troops, with William Pillow in the lead, ran down the path toward the village.

Back at one of the houses, before the troops reached the town, an Indian girl came out and began to grind corn. Then an Indian

brave came out, put one arm around her waist, and began to
help grind the corn. The sight was too much for one of the
hidden riflemen. He drew a bead and fired. The Indian fell dead
at the girl's feet, and she tried desperately to drag his body
into the cabin.

In the town of Nickajack the first shot was fired by Colonel
John Montgomery. It must have been a shot he regretted, for
his bullet went through a crack in a cabin wall and struck an
Indian baby at its mother's breast, killing mother and child.

The firing was general now as the Indians ran from the village
to the river bank and jumped into their canoes. Few escaped
the long rifles, and many were shot in the water.

Joe Brown swam up beside a wounded Indian trying to get
away in a canoe. "I Cherokee," said the Indian, meaning he
was not one of the hostile Chickamaugas.

"What are you doing at Nickajack?"

"Visiting friends."

Brown sank his tomahawk in the Indian's skull.

The Indians from Running Water Town, just seven hundred
yards from where the present highway to Chattanooga crosses
the Tennessee, came running to Nickajack when they heard
the guns. The white men met them in a narrow pass between
mountain and river, and in a few minutes it was all over. Seventy
Indian braves were dead in the two battles, most of them lying
on the river bottom.

The Indian squaws, recognizing Joe Brown as their captive
of years before, were relieved when he told them they would
not be massacred. In the battle at the pass one white man,
Joshua Thomas, received a wound of which he later died—the
only man in the expedition to receive a fatal wound.

Many Indians would have escaped by swimming the river
except for the vigilance of Rains and Mansker, who had not
crossed over. They led a party to cut them off, and the
long rifles did not often miss the heads bobbing in the water.

Nobody saw Jack Civil during the fight, or after it. The soldiers
burned the village and recrossed the Tennessee before night.
They took with them two fresh scalps found at Nickajack,

believed to be those of the Bledsoe boys of Sumner, and for which the Indian chief Breath paid with his life.

On the way home one of the soldiers, perhaps hearing in his dreams the screams of the wounded and dying, climbed a tree in the middle of the night, fell out of it and was killed—all apparently without waking up.

And what of Charles Bosley, the sixteen-year-old soldier? We have no record of what he did at Nickajack, but we can be pretty certain that, being strong and active, he was in the thick of the fight. He found that soldiering agreed with him, and later he became a commander of mounted scouts whose duty it was to protect travelers passing through the wilderness.

Nickajack was just one brief incident in the life of Charles Bosley. He came of a long-lived family. His father died at 104, his brother Beal at 96, his Uncle Elijah at 130, and he himself at 93. The fantastic age of Elijah Bosley was reported in the Nashville *Union and American* in 1870.

Charles outlived his brother, who was older, and also Joe Brown, to become perhaps the last survivor of the Nickajack campaign.

We know that Charles attended the first school taught in Nashville, where he learned to read and write. A few years after Nickajack he moved to Natchez, where he married. His first wife died, and Bosley came back to Nashville where he married again and lived in a large house on Harding Road, then Richland Pike, where Overbrook School now stands.

The boy soldier of the Nickajack campaign settled down to making money and did so well at it that he became one of the richest men in Tennessee, worth a million dollars.

Charles Bosley has not been forgotten. His descendants are still living in Nashville. His only heir, a seven-year-old great-grandchild, Gertrude Bosley Bowling Whitworth, died in 1962 at the age of 99.

Bosley enjoyed yet another distinction. Some time toward the close of his long life he went to Nashville with his wife to visit the photographic establishment of T. F. Saltsman, at the corner of Union and College streets, to have his picture taken.

Charles Bosley

Another memory of Charles Bosley is connected with a stone eagle which stands atop the grave marker of Governor William Carroll in the Old City Cemetery.

Bosley had entered into an agreement to provide the stone for this eagle from his rock quarry. A contractor and his employees, who were free men of color, went out to get the stone.

Bosley had many slaves, and these were soon involved in a controversy with the "free men of color" as to which had the higher or more desirable status. The quarrel soon became a brawl, and Bosley ordered the stonecutter and his laborers off the farm.

The stonecutter went, but in the darkness of the night he came back, the wheels of his oxcart wrapped in blankets and the hooves of his ox padded, lest a clatter break the stillness of the night. While Bosley slept, the stonecutter hauled the stone away on muffled wheels.

Fearing the wrath of Bosley, the stonecutter took a page from
Poe's "Purloined Letter." He hauled his big rock up on the side
of Capitol Hill and lost himself among the many stonecutters
who were shaping stones for the State Capitol, soon to be built.
Thus camouflaged by scores of men with hammer and chisel,
he carved the eagle that stands at Carroll's grave today.

William Wales in the *Southwestern Monthly* (1852) tells us
that where the Bosley house stood there once was another
home—a house of logs with a rock chimney that sent blue smoke
curling against the sky. The building was Johnson's Fort.

Wales reported there were two springs near the early fort—and
they are there today. The one nearest the Bosley house was—and
is—marked by a springhouse, and rises near a little stream which
flows around the base of a craggy hill. This is a chalybeate
or mineral spring, and its waters were once bottled in the
springhouse for medicinal purposes.

The second spring was described by Wales as the Sulphur
Spring "over the ridge beyond Mr. Bosley's" and today it is
around the hill and across the Bosley Springs Road from the
Imperial House Apartments. This spring was a popular "resort"
in its day. Wales wrote in 1852:

"Few of those who unmolested and with fine equipages roll
along the superb gravel turnpike ever think of the thrilling
adventures of Indian murder and outrage which have marked
the vicinity, the tales of which paled the cheeks of their progeni-
tors, the hardy settlers of other times.

"Somewhere about the year 1790," Wales continued, "a fort
called Johnson's Fort stood on the green knoll now occupied
by Mr. Bosley's house." The builder was Isaac Johnson (or
Johnston). The name appears twice among the signers of the
Cumberland Compact. Other accounts say Isaac Johnson, husband of James Robertson's sister Ann, was killed by a falling
tree in the Watauga settlement.

All accounts have it that pioneer John Cockrill was attacked
by an Indian at the Sulphur Spring and pinned under his horse.
He shot the Indian and escaped over the ridge to Johnson's
Fort. He was married to the widow Ann Robertson Johnson—by
his own account—in 1780. This couple later lived beside Cockrill's

Spring, and the big oak which still stands in Centennial Park, where the Natchez Trace passed out of the city.

Two children were killed by Indians beside the "chalybeate" spring, old accounts say, and two others were wounded. The Indians committed other murders here, and for many years a big cherry tree on the lawn marked the spot where a Captain Hunter had met his death.

The dusky killers and their victims are gone, and these are happier times. But if ghosts walk or dreams linger, what better spot than this?

GENERAL JACKSON'S
BRAVE JOURNEY

On great occasions, such as the 150th anniversary of the Battle of New Orleans, the Cornwallis candle at the Hermitage flickers briefly in honor of Andrew Jackson's victory over the British. And every year, on the General's birthday, March 15, wreaths are laid on his grave and solemn ceremonies honor the memory of a great Tennessean.

General Jackson's trip to the Gulf Coast, three years after his return to the Hermitage from Washington, is a dramatic and little-known chapter of his life. It offers a close-up example of the raw courage and indomitable character of the former president.

Jackson was 73 years old and a man beset on all sides. The repose he longed to find at the Hermitage eluded him because he was burdened with many problems. It didn't come until he slept in the quiet garden.

He had to contend with the deep, unending, and incurable indebtedness of his adopted son, Andrew Jackson, Jr. General Jackson, almost without financial resources himself, never failed to assume these debts and pay them at great sacrifice. Frequent failure of the Hermitage Plantation cotton crop added to his financial woes.

He was in bad health. It is likely that the illnesses that took his life five years later had already set in. He had to frequently be bled by his doctors.

The Democratic party was in deep trouble. Even some of

183

Jackson's oldest friends could not and would not vote again
for his protege President Martin Van Buren.

On December 19, 1839, Jackson wrote to his former ward,
Andrew Hutchings:

"You have seen the pressing invitation of the citizens of New
Orleans that I should be with them on the 8th of January.
The pressing solicitation of my friends, though weak and
afflicted, has induced me to agree to make the attempt. Circumstances of a private and imperious nature induce me also to
make the attempt."

The "private and imperious" circumstances to which he referred was the financial thicket in which Andrew, Jr., had become
hopelessly entangled and from which neither he nor his
father would ever escape.

On Christmas Eve, with snow clouds flying in the north,
Jackson drew a draft on his cotton crop to apply on Junior's
debts and pay his own travel expenses to New Orleans. Indica-
tions are that his expenses were later reimbursed by citizens
of that city.

The Cumberland River was low for the time of year, so General Jackson left Nashville in a carriage. Since steamboats could
not come up river—because of low water at Harpeth Shoals—he
set out for Smithland, Kentucky, where the Cumberland empties
into the Ohio.

General Jackson was in a hurry, and his manner of travel
paid scant regard to comfort. From morning until evening halt
he did not leave the carriage, nor did it stop. The first day
he made twenty-nine miles, the second forty, the third thirty-
nine, and the fourth twenty-seven, placing him in the vicinity
of Smithland.

On the last day of the month, as he was leaving Smithland
aboard the steamboat Gallatin, he wrote:

"From the mouth of the Ohio we have been struggling in
floating ice. We have been in the midst of falling snow for
twenty-four hours, not being able to sail at night. I am not
so well this morning, but hope to be better when the weather
changes. . . ."

The General kept busy. He made arrangements for the baling

and shipping of his cotton and for the installation of a grist
mill. At Memphis he was met by the steamer Vicksburg, sent
up by the state of Mississippi, and here he stopped to arrange
a new line of financial credit to relieve Junior's debts. Farther
down river, at his Halcyon Plantation, he again paused to settle
or stretch out payments on debts. A letter to Andrew, Jr.,
revealed Jackson's thoughts:

"I hope for the better, and when the worse comes we must
try somehow to meet (it). I hope all these things will result
to your benefit in the end, and be a shield to prevent you
hereafter from running in debt for things useless to your comfort
or prosperity or that of your little family. Recollect my son
that I have taken this trip to endeavor to relieve you from
present embarrassments, and if I live to realize it, I will die
contented in the hope that you will never again encumber
yourself with debt, that may result in the poverty of yourself
and little family of so much promise, and whom I so much
love. I pray you keep in mind that it will require all our economy
to meet next year and pay the money I have borrowed from
Mr. William Nichol."

Writing to Postmaster General Amos Kendall, Jackson described what happened to him at Vicksburg:

"Having undertaken the journey, I was determined to get
through, or fall in the struggle. I have long found that complain-
ing never eased pain. I therefore put on a calm face, but my
dear sir I suppose I was taken with hemorrhage the morning
before I reached Vicksburg, and the only remedy I had was
common salt.

"The next day I traveled to Jackson, the seat of government,
and spent two nights and one day there. I returned to Vicksburg
and took a boat the next morning, and struggled against pain
and sickness for ten days and nights. Still Providence, as usual,
took care of me."

While Jackson, with the aid of Providence, traveled down river,
the people of New Orleans were in the throes of preparation
for the visit of the old hero. And as one might expect, politics
reared its head.

Jackson's political enemies in New Orleans were the Whigs,

and they were led by Balie Peyton, whom Jackson knew well, a former member of the Congress from Sumner County, Tennessee. The editor of the *Picayune* was a Whig who had opposed Jackson "from the first jump out," but he wanted politics forgotten during the visit. "We should like to see political and party feeling left in abeyance for that one day," he wrote. "Indeed," he added, "we think that these feelings should never be permitted to interrupt the harmony of social life, or the interchange of civilities between man and man."

That was too broad a view for some Whigs. In the legislature A. M. Brashear asserted that "the whole thing was a political move, got up to subserve Van Buren and his party." He further charged that Jackson's visit "encouraged 'man worship' which proceeded originally from Washington and not from the people of New Orleans."

A Jackson man got up and said he would rather worship a Jackson, a Bonaparte, or a Cromwell than a man sitting on his moneybags with a quill behind his ear—a man whose greatness lay in the gold which filled his pockets.

But it was a small incident. The great day came, and as Jackson's steamboat touched the shore, the city went wild with excitement. The *New Orleans Courier* reported:

"The celebration of the Eighth of January which took place here yesterday will not be forgotten while memory holds good among the thousands and tens of thousands who witnessed it. It was not a triumphal entry such as the Romans celebrated. . . . Nor could the celebration be compared to a modern fete in Europe where the sovereign has to case his body in armament, or shut himself in a ball-proof carriage. No, the whole scene was one befitting a free people, and worthy of the veteran who is first in the hearts of his countrymen."

The *Picayune* reported that "it was a day that will be remembered while New Orleans stands and the Mississippi flows."

This Whig newspaper continued:

"The reception generally was one of which the aged veteran should be proud. There was a lukewarmness on the part of some of his political opponents which we consider anything but praiseworthy. But the body of our people were out."

Along Canal Street the iron-trimmed balconies were "groaning with fair burthens—ladies waving their handkerchiefs while the silver headed warrior bowed."

Through the dense throng the old soldier rode to the Place d'Armes, now Jackson Square. A military guard ushered him into the St. Louis Cathedral, where Rev. Abbe Anduze delivered an address of welcome in English and French.

Later, in the square, Jackson reviewed the troops and veterans of 1814-15, while a cannon boomed salutes. A *Picayune* reporter wrote that "the light of other days could be seen brightening the old soldier's eyes as he contemplated the fine martial display." That evening the general and his suite attended a comedy at the St. Charles theater.

This statue of General Jackson stands beside St. Louis Cathedral in Jackson Square, New Orleans, Louisiana.

It had been a great day—but there was a foul-up. Reported the *Picayune:*

"Some thousands of our citizens, a goodly host, made a pilgrimage to the battleground yesterday, as in duty bound, to see General Jackson and witness the ceremony of laying the cornerstone. They came away as wise as they went, the old hero not being able to attend.

"There were steamboats, towboats, flatboats, railroad cars, coaches, cabs, cabriolets, hacks, horses, wagons, sandcarts, gocarts, handcarts, drays, dugouts—in short every description of land carriage and water craft, in requisition to transport the immense throng. Big bugs in buggies, . . . high people and low people, fat folks and funny folks. In short all orders were there, marching in admitted disorder to the battlefield. They went quietly to their homes . . . consoling themselves with the thought that if the cornerstone wasn't laid, it should have been."

The matter of the cornerstone was never settled. Jackson did finally go to the battlefield, but the day was rainy, and he was accompanied by a relatively small group, including a number of veterans.

On the last day of his visit, en route to the steamer, he did lay a cornerstone in the square. The monument was finally erected on the battlefield, and whether it contains this stone is a matter of conjecture.

The *Courier* reported another incident of the visit:

"On Saturday the General expressed a wish to see the free men of color who were at the line in 1814-15. A large number of them attended at his hotel, where they were kindly received by the General. They were introduced by General Plauche:

" 'The brave soldiers who fought in defense of the country under the orders of Majors Lacoste and Daquin, wish to present their respects, and beg the honor of shaking hands with the general as a token of their gratitude. They pray God to bless you and prolong your existence.' "

At some time during his visit General Jackson sat for his portrait, perhaps while receiving callers in his rooms. One of these, by Amans, hangs at Brown University in Providence, Rhode Island. Three portraits are believed to have been painted

This portrait of General Jackson, his spectacles pushed high upon his forehead, is believed to have been painted in New Orleans in 1840.

by Lafosse during or soon after Jackson's visit, with perhaps one original and two copies. In one, a pastel, Jackson's eyes are tinted brown, though most accounts say he had blue eyes and—in younger days—red hair.

The Lafosse pastel is of a man beset, as Jackson was at the time. The compressed lips, set jaw, and somber eyes—one slightly different from the other—tell the story of Jackson's journey better than words can do. Lafosse, indeed, caught a suffering man who was "putting on a calm face."

On his way back home, Andrew Jackson again traveled through river ice and caught a heavy cold. "We reached Nashville on February 1," he wrote, "where we were kindly greeted by numerous friends and the whole legislature in a body. I am now reclining under the peaceful roof of the Hermitage with my dear little family. My cold has somewhat increased since I got home, through a little imprudence."

As General Jackson had believed, Providence had taken care of him again.

FORT DONELSON:
The Confederates Fought Well

During the long summer and autumn of 1861, after Tennessee seceded from the Union, Nashville stirred and bustled as the new arsenal of the Southern states.

The death and defeat of Nashville's own General Felix Zollicoffer at Fishing Creek brought the war home, but Middle Tennessee felt secure behind the Confederate lines of General Albert Sidney Johnston. The war still seemed far away, but the Tennessee and Cumberland rivers were twin arteries leading to the heart of the Confederacy, and Federal commanders in the West knew it. During the winter the Federals were busy building armed gunboats on the Ohio.

Tennessee Governor Isham G. Harris also recognized the danger. He ordered General Daniel S. Donelson to locate forts on the two rivers at the best points below the Kentucky line. Fort Donelson, named for the general, was located on a bluff at Dover, on the west side of the Cumberland and eighty-seven miles northwest of Nashville. It had water batteries commanding the river. The Wynn's Ferry Road ran south from Dover to Charlotte and Nashville.

Eleven miles away, on the east bank of the Tennessee River, Fort Henry, named for Confederate Senator Gustavus A. Henry, was built almost on the water line, where it could be flooded by any spring rise. Work on the two forts proceeded slowly, and Confederate officers found Nashvillians unwilling to supply slave labor. "The need of fortifying Nashville," wrote historian Stanley Horn, "was laughed at." But it was no laughing matter.

191

Aside from the two little forts, Nashville was an undefended city. And early in February two Union officers, General Ulysses S. Grant and Commodore Andrew H. Foote, teamed up in an army-navy operation intended to take and occupy the forts.

It was an amphibious attack that was to set the pattern for many more to come, in this and other wars. Foote landed seventeen thousand men on both sides of the river near the fort, then he steamed his gunboats up to the Confederate bastions and opened fire. It was short work. General Lloyd Tilghman had sent his garrison of three thousand to Fort Donelson, but he had returned to Fort Henry to share the fate of a tiny detachment of artillery, less than sixty men, left to duel with the gunboats. The odds were soon reduced to four Confederate cannons against fifty-four on the boats, and after two hours of bombardment, Tilghman surrendered.

Foote's cutter, sent to receive the surrender, sailed right into the fort on the rising water. As one historian remarked, if the gunboats had not taken the fort, its guns would have been silenced by flood water.

After the surrender of Fort Henry, Grant turned his thoughts to an attack on Fort Donelson, believing it would be another easy victim. He was mistaken. Reports on the strength of the Confederate garrison vary, from fifteen thousand to twenty-one thousand men. It was commanded by three ill-assorted brigadier generals. They were John B. Floyd, a political general technically in command, Gideon J. Pillow, and Simon B. Buckner.

Various writers hold that Floyd was incompetent, Pillow was pretentious and bombastic, and Buckner was suffering from an attack of severe pessimism. At any rate the trio managed to lose the fort to a force that was, for part of the time, no larger than their own and despite the fact that the Confederate soldiers were successful in every mission given them during the battle.

The land surrounding Fort Donelson and Dover was rough and wooded, cut by high ridges and deep valleys of several creeks. These were swollen by high water, and it was difficult for Grant's army to invest the fort. On February 13, the Federals attacked the center of the Confederate line and were driven back with heavy loss.

This drawing from Harper's Weekly, March 8, 1962, shows the Confederate assault on the Federal right wing on the morning of the last day of the battle at Fort Donelson. According to Harper's the fourth attack on Schwartz's battery was successful.

Stanley Horn writes that the suffering that night was one of the ghastliest chapters of the war. "Artillery . . . had set the woods afire . . . with the coming of darkness those who had escaped death by burning were exposed to the danger of death from freezing . . . War that night was truly hell—a bloody, freezing hell on earth."

Meanwhile Foote's gunboat flotilla had steamed down the Tennessee from Fort Henry, entered the Ohio, and turned up the Cumberland. On the fourteenth, Foote steamed right up to the muzzles of the Confederate water batteries, expecting a repetition of his easy victory at Fort Henry. But the Confederate gunners laid to their work, and at close range their shells "peeled the armor off the gunboats like taking the bark off trees." Out of 370 shots fired during the battle, the Confederates scored 180 hits, damaging every vessel and severely wounding Foote. The flotilla was forced to retire.

Grant's force had now grown to twenty-seven thousand men. Both armies were suffering from exposure and cold, and the trio of Confederate generals thought they were being squeezed against the river in a trap from which they must escape. Accordingly, the Confederate left, under Pillow and Forrest, struck the Federal right, under McClernand, and drove it back against the center in a furious and bitter battle, clearing the road south to Nashville.

The Confederates could have continued the attack or marched to Nashville. But because of command failure and a poorly concerted battle plan, they did neither. Grant, who had been visiting the wounded Foote aboard one of the gunboats, returned to find his army in a precarious position. He reasoned that the Confederates had weakened their right wing and upon attacking proved this to be the case. A part of the Confederate earthwork was captured.

Meanwhile the victorious Confederates on the left returned to the fort. Soon the situation was just as it had been before, with nothing gained from the bloody sally. That night the brigadiers, discouraged by high water on the escape roads and the exhaustion and exposure of the men, decided to surrender. Floyd passed the command to Pillow, and then escaped, with his four Virginia regiments, across the river. Pillow then passed the command to Buckner and also made good his escape in an abandoned scow.

Buckner then proceeded to give up the fort to General Grant, who demanded "unconditional surrender"—and got it. In the great roundup of eleven thousand prisoners, the Federals missed Colonel Nathan Bedford Forrest, who rode out through the icy backwaters with his whole command, not losing a man. "I will bust hell wide open," said Forrest, "before I will stay here and see them surrender."

General Bushrod Johnson, another Confederate, just walked away to freedom. In the confusion, nobody noticed.

The forts had fallen, and the stars of Grant and Forrest rose from that day. Nashville was a doomed city, swept first by wild rumors and later by panic as the Bluecoat armies drew near.

EARLY EDITORS SHOT IT OUT

The life of a newspaperman may be no bed of roses—especially if he is trying to cover the proceedings of the Tennessee legislature. But there has been a time in Nashville when editors wore guns and used them to settle their personal and political differences.

Four times between 1852 and 1908 the sound of gunfire has echoed in city streets as editors battled other editors or fought to defend themselves from irate readers. Two of the duels were fought in the 1850s.

Zollicoffer Vs. Marling

Felix Kirk Zollicoffer, boss and "kingmaker" of the powerful Whig party in Tennessee in 1852, was not a man to take an insult lightly. A native of Maury County, he began his newspaper career at Paris, Tennessee.

Zollicoffer moved to Nashville to become editor of the *Republican Banner,* the official Whig organ in the state. He had masterminded the successful campaign of Lean Jimmy Jones against Democrat James K. Polk for governor. In 1852 the *Banner* was going all out in support of General Winfield (Old Fuss-and-Feathers) Scott for President, while the Nashville *Union* was supporting Democratic nominee Franklin Pierce.

John Leake Marling, editor of the *Union,* was an aggressive

197

political writer, and on August 20, 1852, at the height of the
campaign, Marling wrote:

"A plain word or two to the *Banner*. It has pursued a reckless
and most unscrupulous course towards General Pierce. It has
tried to identify him with the abolitionism of New Hampshire.
. . . It has tried to misrepresent his sentiments on slavery. .
. . Now we say this is BELIEING General Pierce. We use the
word in all its length and breadth. . . ."

That was enough for Zollicoffer. As he saw it, Marling had
called him a liar and that wasn't all. A new bridge was to be
built across the Cumberland. Marling wanted the bridge at the
foot of Broad Street. Zollicoffer, according to his biographer,
Raymond E. Myers, wanted the bridge at the corner of the
square. His reason, Marling charged, was self interest.

When Zollicoffer read the editorial that morning, he took down
his duelling pistols, and his wife helped prepare them for action.
"I had rather see him dead," she told a neighbor, "than dishon-
ored."

Marling was known as a brave man and a good shot, but
Zollicoffer went about his business. He presented himself in front
of the *Union* office at the corner of Cherry and Cedar (now
Fourth and Charlotte) with pistol in hand. Marling, not a man
to hesitate, ran into the street with a revolver. All at once the
sidewalks were empty, and the fight was on.

Marling fired first and missed. Zollicoffer pulled the trigger,
but his old-fashioned duelling pistol misfired. He calmly
reached into his vest pocket for a fresh cap and "put it on the
nipper" according to Judge James T. Bell. Marling held his fire
while Zollicoffer was doing this Bell recalled, but a moment
later the pistols popped again and Marling fell, seriously
wounded in the face.

Other accounts say Marling fired while Zollicoffer was replac-
ing his percussion cap, wounding Zollicoffer in his pistol hand.
Zollicoffer himself, in writing a report of the incident, said: "We
do not distinctly remember the order of the shots," and did
not mention that he was wounded.

The next year Zollicoffer was elected to Congress, where he
served three terms. He never returned to his editor's chair.

Marling, having recovered from his wound, became U.S. Minister to Guatemala. Years after the duel, Bell said, Marling's wound hastened his death.

Marling and Zollicoffer were reconciled and became friends. Eight years after the duel Zollicoffer, a Confederate general leading his troops into action, was killed at Fishing Creek.

Poindexter Vs. Hall

On the morning of November 19, 1859, the Nashville *Union and American* appeared with "column rules turned upside down" making heavy black lines between the columns. It was, in those days, a newspaper's way of announcing an important death. A brief notice inside the paper read:

"The sad duty devolves upon us of announcing the death of our associate and friend, G. G. Poindexter. He was killed yesterday morning by Allen A. Hall, the editor of the *Daily News.*"

George Gilmer Poindexter, a native of Virginia, was a graduate of Bowdoin College, Maine, and Cumberland University Law School, Lebanon, Tennessee. He came to Nashville as an unknown young man and within a year was the "principal editor" of the *Union and American* and a partner in the paper.

Allen A. Hall was a veteran editor of the Nashville *Daily News,* a newspaper of Whig leanings established in 1857. Hall was fifty-seven when he killed Poindexter.

Poindexter and his newspaper defended slavery. John Bell had attacked the "peculiar institution," and Hall defended Bell. In 1834—in a more liberal and less heated atmosphere—Hall had said slavery must end. Poindexter now upbraided him for such sentiments, and Hall said his remarks were taken out of context—they represented the sentiment of the people "at the time."

One thing led to another until Poindexter charged that Hall's editorials were "utterly destitute of truth" and that the older man was "an editor who utters calumnies against a contemporary trusting to the supposed privileges of age to shield him from responsibility."

Hall replied in kind, and the affair was well on its way. The first clash came between Poindexter and Hall's son, but no shots were fired and no harm done.

Poindexter, armed and accompanied by an armed friend, called at Hall's office. Hall wasn't in, and Poindexter left. A short time later, as Poindexter walked alone on Cherry Street near the News office, Hall stepped into the street carrying a double-barreled shotgun loaded with buckshot. Poindexter, walking up hill in a light rain, was carrying an umbrella. He did not know Hall by sight.

"Stop, Sir!" cried Hall. He repeated it twice, at the same time raising his weapon to his shoulder. Poindexter did not stop, and the roar of the shotgun filled the street. The young man, riddled by shot, fell to the pavement. Beside him lay his broken umbrella, and a loaded pistol he had tried to draw too late.

A vast array of citizens turned out for Poindexter's funeral at the First Baptist Church, though the young man was still almost a stranger in Nashville. Horn's brass band led the procession, and editors and reporters of the *Union and American* wore black crepe on their hats. Poindexter was buried at Clarksville, where he had lived briefly before coming to Nashville.

Attorney General William B. Bate, who was to become a Confederate general in the Civil War, pleaded powerfully that Hall be brought to trial, but the record does not show that Hall was ever tried. He apparently supported the Union when war came, and in 1863 he got his reward. Abraham Lincoln made him minister to Bolivia, where he remained until his death in 1868.

Banks Shoots Littleton

"A hot encounter" was the headline in the Nashville *American* on Christmas morning, 1887, "High Street the Scene of a Fierce Fusillade."

The story was an account of another shooting in which a shotgun had taken its toll on the streets of Nashville. Young John J. Littleton, fiery editor of the *National Review*, the state's official Republican newspaper, had been shot by Joe Banks, Nashville real estate dealer. The shooting, early on the morning of Christmas Eve, had taken place near the High Street (Sixth Avenue) entrance to the Watkins Institute. The shots were fired from a small house across the street owned by John Cockrell.

Both men were Republicans, and Littleton had been defeated in a race for mayor of Nashville early that fall. He had attacked Banks in the *National Review*, using language the *American* refused to repeat.

Littleton did not die at once from his wounds but walked most of the way to his home, where he lived for four days. Dr. Nichol told him: "Well, John, there is no hope for you. These wounds are fatal."

In a statement printed in the *American*, Littleton said: "I heard a shot fired from behind me. Quick as thought I felt a shock. That shot felled me to the ground. I had a revolver, but my arm was filled with shot so I couldn't use it.

"I said, 'that is enough, don't fire again.' He fired two shots into my legs. I raised up and saw Joe Banks. He broke and ran. I said, 'watch the coward run from a dead man.' Then I cried, 'oh my wife and child.'"

Littleton lived long enough to see his father, who came from Texas. Before he died he told members of his family he had forgiven the man who took his life.

Banks was put in jail, along with Cockrell, who was referred to by the *American* as the "Buzzard Orator." Neither Banks nor Cockrell were convicted of the shooting.

The *American* commented: "That it was a fearful tragedy there can be no doubt. That it was the outgrowth of a line of journalism peculiar to Mr. Littleton there can be little question. . . . It is well that the parties were of the same political faith."

Less than thirty years old, Littleton had been elected to the state legislature and was at the time of his death secretary and treasurer of the state executive committee of the Republican party.

Cooper Kills Carmack

The killing of Edward Ward Carmack by Robin Cooper in 1908 is still remembered by older citizens. It widened the gulf between two camps—"Carmack" and "Patterson"—and affected the political history of Tennessee for years afterward.

Carmack, a militant leader for the cause of prohibition, had been a U.S. senator and a crusading editor of the Memphis *Commercial Appeal.* In the summer of 1908 he waged a colorful campaign for governor against Malcolm R. (Ham) Patterson.

Patterson won the nomination by seven thousand votes, and Carmack was then called to be editor of *The Nashville Tennessean.* A recent history of Tennessee says he brought to the editor's chair "his ardor for prohibition, his uncanny ability to express his thoughts with brilliant bitterness, and the courage to write his convictions."

Carmack soon charged a political alliance between Governor Patterson and ex-Governor John I. Cox, formerly political enemies. The man he credited with effecting this alliance was Colonel Duncan Cooper, Patterson's personal and political friend.

On November 8, 1908, the *Tennessean* printed an editorial written by Carmack called "The Diplomat of the Zweibund." In it Carmack referred to the man "who grafted the dead bough to the living tree and made it bloom, who made playmates of the lion and leopard . . . to Major Duncan Brown Cooper, the great diplomat of the political Zweibund, be all honor and glory forever." A filler below the editorial read: "Thou shalt not yoke the ox with the ass"—a plain reference to Patterson and Cox.

This would not appear to be shooting language but Colonel Cooper was offended, and that afternoon when Carmack walked up the hill from his editorial office the Coopers met him. Both were armed and the editor was also carrying a pistol. Carmack was in the act of raising his hat and speaking to Mrs. Charles

H. Eastman when the Coopers accosted him. Mrs. Eastman said the encounter took place just south of the entrance to the Polk Flats, now Seventh Avenue North south of Union Street. Mrs. Eastman quoted Colonel Cooper:

"Now we've got you all right, sir. We've got the drop on you."

Carmack sprang toward the edge of the pavement, reaching for his pistol. There was a volley of shots, and the editor fell dead. He was shot three times from the revolver of Robin Cooper. The older Cooper apparently did not fire. Two empty shells were found in Carmack's revolver, and the younger Cooper was wounded in the shoulder.

Enoch Mitchell, in his recent history of Tennessee, says, "It appears that the editor fired the first shot. However, Carmack partisans have never acknowledged such to be the case." Evidence showed that Carmack was taken by surprise by the Coopers, who in their own words had "the drop" on him.

The Coopers were found guilty of murder by a Davidson County jury, but the Tennessee Supreme Court remanded the case of Robin Cooper to the lower court, where the charges were nolle prosequi or dropped. The elder Cooper was pardoned by Governor Patterson.

After a number of years, Robin Cooper died a violent death.

In his death Carmack gained the end he sought. Prohibition came to Tennessee the next year, steam-rollered over Patterson's veto by an irate legislature. And the brilliant orator, Ham Patterson, would never again be governor. In 1932, aging but not forgotten, he tried it again against Hill McAllister and Lewis Pope. But the people remembered 1908, and Ham Patterson went down to defeat.

A SHOOTOUT ON THE SQUARE

In 1812 many great events happened in Tennessee.

In the winter of 1811-12 earthquakes shook the land. Lightning seemed to flash from the ground, dull explosions were heard, earth tremors changed the course of the Mississippi River, and overnight Reelfoot Lake was formed.

The settlements were shaken by news of war against Great Britain. That great patriot of the frontier, Andrew Jackson, called for volunteers. "Shall we, who have clamoured for war, now skulk into a corner? Are we the titled slaves of George III? The military conscripts of Napoleon? Or the frozen peasants of the Russian Czar? No! . . ." From Cragfont, in Sumner County, General James Winchester wrote Jackson that graybeard veterans of the Revolution were drilling in the open fields.

But what shook Nashville hardest was a fight—or brawl—on the public square.

It all started on the way back from Jackson's Natchez expedition. Not having seen any Redcoats, Jackson's officers started quarreling among themselves. At the bottom of the trouble was the brigade inspector, a young Nashville hardware merchant named William Carroll, who would one day be governor of Tennessee. Jackson thought highly of him. However, Jackson's biographer, James Parton, was not kind to Carroll. He wrote: "He was a tall, well-formed man, much given to military affairs, and thus attracted the notice of General Jackson, who advanced him so rapidly, and paid him such marked attentions, as to procure for the young stranger a great many enemies.

"Carroll, moreover, was not a genuine son of the wilderness.

205

With all his powerful frame and superior stature, there was
an expression of delicacy in his smooth, fair countenance that
found small favor in the eyes of the rougher pioneers. Perhaps,
too, in those days, there was a touch of dandyism in his attire
and demeanor . . . . Captain William Carroll had his enemies
among the young officers of General Jackson's division."

After reaching Nashville after the march from Natchez, Carroll was challenged to a duel by a young lieutenant who
"thought proper to consider himself insulted." Carroll declined
on the ground that the lieutenant was not a gentleman. Jesse
Benton, the bearer of the note, then challenged Carroll. This
time, the challenge was accepted.

Less famous than his brother, Colonel Thomas Hart Benton,
Jesse Benton was a descendant from an old North Carolina
family. The brothers had lived on a farm south of Nashville
on the Natchez Trace. Jesse moved to Nashville and gained
some prominence in the community, while Thomas was a leading
member of the bar in Franklin.

Captain Carroll asked Jackson to be his second in the duel
with Jesse Benton. At first the General declined, saying he was
too old for that sort of thing. But when Carroll said there was
a group of young men who were jealous of his commission, and
conspiring to run him out of the country, Jackson got his dander
up. He agreed to serve as Carroll's second.

"You needn't fear Jesse Benton," Jackson assured Carroll.
"He couldn't hit you if you were broad as a barn door."

The men stood just ten feet apart, firing big one-ounce balls
from their single-shot dueling pistols. Jesse fired first, and sure
enough he missed Carroll, or almost did, drawing but a drop
of blood from the captain's thumb.

Now it was Carroll's turn to fire. While looking into the muzzle
of that big pistol, Jesse Benton adopted a strategy that gave
Tennesseans a good laugh for years to come. He bent over and
presented the best padded part of his anatomy as a target.
Carroll fired, inflicting a wound that made it impossible for Jesse
to sit comfortably for some time. As Marquis James wrote, the
spirit was more wounded than the flesh.

Meanwhile, Thomas Hart Benton returned from Washington

where he had been laboring to straighten out General Jackson's financial accounts with the government. When he heard that his old commander had seconded another man in a duel with his brother, he got mad. Benton said harsh things about Jackson, and the gossips who reported to the General made them sound even worse. Jackson's patience, never very durable, snapped. He publicly announced he would horsewhip Tom Benton.

Before many days passed Jackson heard the Bentons were in Nashville at the City Hotel on the public square. That same day Jackson and John Coffee rode to town and put up at the Nashville Inn, also on the square.

The next morning at nine o'clock Jackson and Coffee walked across the square to the post office to get their mail. Both were armed, and Jackson carried a riding whip. Crossing the square they spied Tom Benton standing on the porch of the City Hotel. Coming back the two men took the sidewalk, and Jackson walked up to Tom Benton, who had been joined by his brother. Jackson raised his whip and roared: "Now, you damned rascal, I am going to punish you. Defend yourself."

Benton reached for a pistol but Jackson beat him to the draw and pointed his pistol at Tom's heart. Benton started backing into the hotel, his hand still in his coat. Jackson followed him, but did not fire.

Meanwhile, Jesse Benton, seeing his brother covered, fired at Jackson from the rear and dropped him with a severe bullet wound in the shoulder. As he was falling, Jackson fired at Tom Benton but missed him, the powder burning Benton's sleeve. Coffee, a little slow to get into the action, charged through the smoke and fired at Tom Benton, who was again in luck as the hasty shot missed. Coffee clubbed his pistol and came on. Benton's pistols were empty, and just as it appeared Coffee would beat his brains out Benton stepped backward into an open staircase and fell headlong to the floor below. Thinking Tom Benton disposed of, Coffee turned to help Jackson, who was bleeding heavily from the wound Jesse Benton had given him.

In the meantime Stockley Hays, a nephew of Rachel Jackson, "just happened" to appear on the scene. He drew a sword cane and plunged it straight at Jesse Benton's heart. Hays' delicate blade hit a big button on Jesse Benton's coat and snapped in two. Jesse, finding himself still alive, pushed the muzzle of his second pistol against Hays' chest and pulled the trigger. The gun failed to fire.

Hays, assisted by Captain Hammond, then threw Jesse to the floor and, drawing a knife, strove to cut his throat. Jesse caught his sleeve, however, and held on for dear life. At length Hays wrested his arm free, but just as he raised the knife for a fatal stroke, his hand was caught from behind by a bystander, and Jesse's life was saved. In his own account of the brawl, published several days later in a Franklin newspaper, Tom Benton said he received several slight knife wounds from Coffee and Alexander Donaldson, not mentioned in Coffee's account.

After the fight the prostrate Jackson was taken to his room, where it was said his blood "soaked two mattresses." For nineteen years he carried Jesse Benton's bullet in his shoulder, finally having it cut out in 1832 during his first term as president.

In the meantime Tom Benton found Jackson's small sword on the floor of the hotel where it had been dropped. He took it on the public square and broke it across his knee, bellowing for Jackson, whom he believed to be unhurt, to come out and continue the fight. It was Tom Benton's last opportunity to crow for some time, because Jackson, as he usually did, won the verdict of public opinion. The day after the fight Benton wrote in Nashville:

"I am literally in hell here. . . . All the puppies of Jackson are at work on me. I see no alternative but to kill or be killed. . . . The fact that I and my brother defeated him and his tribe and broke his small sword in the public square will forever rankle in his bosom."

The Creek uprising and the massacre at Fort Mims made people forget the fight. At the Hermitage, Jackson, still in bed with his wound, said, "By the eternal these people must be saved." Before the federal government knew what had happened, Coffee's cavalry was forming. James reported that Jackson wrote, propped against a pillow: "The health of your general is restored. He will command in person."

Andrew Jackson went on to fame and the presidency of the

United States. Thomas Hart Benton, finding the ladder of success blocked in Tennessee, went to Missouri where he became
a great United States senator. He and Jackson, across the years,
again were friends. But Jesse Benton? He never forgave Jackson,
and he never forgave Tom for forgiving him. He finally took
off to Mississippi for a few years of peace (it is hoped) before
he died.

Tennessee's Natural Bridge.

TENNESSEE'S NATURAL BRIDGE

On the south fork of the Buffalo River, nestled in the Big Bend of the Tennessee, stands Tennessee's Natural Bridge. Until 1930, when Highway 64 bridged the big river, the spot was practically inaccessible to travelers. The nearest town is Waynesboro.

Once Indian hunters and warriors smoked their pipes on the natural terrace of stone seats by the big bluff. And in later years the county courts of Hardin and Wayne held their sessions in the "Rock Courthouse." The most famous judge of this period was William Burrell Walker, whose descendants still visit the spot.

In 1957 the motion picture, "Natchez Trail," was filmed at the Natural Bridge with a fanfare of bright lights and a galaxy of actors from Hollywood. The film starred Zachary Scott, Marcia Henderson, and Bill Campbell. Based on the life of the bandit, John Murrell, it was supposed to end with the villain being pulled apart by four horses. The scene proved too difficult, however, and the unfortunate fellow was disposed of by bashing his head with a rock.

In those days the Alpine Lodge at Natural Bridge was a busy place, with such beauties as Marica Henderson and her supporting cast adding to the scenery. Today, however, the lodge is closed to the public. But not for long. The Natural Bridge Scenic Development Corporation is building a new motel at the site, and the seventies will see new activity under the great bridge where Murrell skulked and the Indians danced their war dance.

211

TRAPPED

Wild buffalo and deer no longer raced through Nashville by 1788, historian A. W. Putnam recorded. The bustling, nine-year-old village on the bluffs was "under fence," and town lots were being sold for "four pounds lawful money of North Carolina."

Besides the six or eight log houses, "sixteen feet square, eight feet clear in the pitch, there might be seen, in different directions among the cedars, ten or fifteen open shanties and a few wagon and bark tents."

It was a fairly prosperous village but not a peaceful one. Almost everywhere Indian tracks were seen very near to the town, but the Indians were certainly concealed in the cane. They had stolen corn from almost every crib, and to catch them the settlers set huge, vicious wolf traps.

In a crib near Eaton's Station (just across the Cumberland) several casks of beans were stored, from which it was believed the Indians had been helping themselves by inserting an arm through cracks in the logs. A wolf trap was set in the beans and chained to the logs inside.

Sure enough there was a howling and caterwauling in the middle of the night, and aroused settlers rushed to the crib. When they reached the scene their jaws dropped in amazement. It was not an Indian who had been caught with his hand in the beans. It was a white man—one of their own number. The

213

thief was caught with his arm in the crack, and it took two men to loosen the cruel iron jaws of the wolf trap.

"That broken arm required splints and bandages," Putnam wrote, "and that poor, lazy white man did not remain many months thereafter in the Cumberland settlements." And as for the Indians "they never caught one," Putnam recorded, "but they lost several traps."

WILSON COUNTY:
A Colorful Past

Historic springs, early churches, and old campgrounds are a part of the past and present of Wilson County.

Just beyond the western border of Lebanon, Hickory Ridge looks down on the valley to the east. Here was one of the earliest settlements in the region. Here Professor George MacWhirter taught school in the Campbell Academy in the early years of the last century.

The Hickory Ridge Methodist Church, also known as Bethlehem Church, which dates back to the early 1800s, is still an active congregation. Reverend John Brooks, a stern and powerful Methodist preacher of his day, was the traveling preacher serving this church about 1820. In his autobiography, Brooks tells of a bitter division in the church.

John Carr wrote that "the very looks of a Methodist preacher were enough to strike terror to a sinner's heart." But Brooks was not able to break the ice. His pleas for peace and reunion fell on deaf ears.

Clarissa Babb, a member of one of the prominent families in the church, rose from her seat and, with tears in her eyes, pleaded with the members for friendship and fellowship. A woman speaking in church was unheard of in that day, but Clarissa won them over. Weeping for joy, the members fell into one another's arms, and all was forgiven.

In the summer of 1792, after their raid on Zeigler's Station, the Indians fled, with their captives, up Barton's Creek, which runs just west of Lebanon, and Town Creek, which runs through the heart of town. John Carr wrote, in his *Early Times in Middle*

215

Tennessee, that the Indians stopped briefly "high up on Spring Creek" to smoke their pipes and make moccasins for the children they had captured. "There was that much of kindness in them," Carr wrote.

The fleeing Indians and their captives, and later their pursuers, also stopped at Martin's Spring, which is still running. The rock spring house may be the oldest structure built by white men in the county. According to Carr, the Indians cut their symbols, and white men cut their initials, on beech trees near the spring.

Doak's Cross Roads, south of Lebanon, had the first church and school in the community, according to Goodspeed. It was probably the first settled community. Its Spring Creek Presbyterian Church was the first in the county, founded in 1801.

Spring Creek runs through Greenwood, now a "lost town." Near this old town site in a bend of Spring Creek, is the location of a prehistoric Indian village. The great mound, typical of these ancient villages, still exists. It is about fifteen feet high and surrounded by smaller mounds. The mound was excavated in 1877 by Professor F. W. Putnam, curator of the Peabody Museum at Harvard University. Putnam sank a shaft from the center of the mound to its base, but all he found was a cedar pole.

Fine pipes and pottery have been found in the village site. In the 1930s a number of strange and valuable sandstone images were found. These figures, with paint pigment still on their eyes and lips, have been exhibited in various museums. One, exhibited at the Museum of Modern Art in New York City, was called "the finest piece of prehistoric sculpture ever found in North America." Two of the images are owned by the University of Tennessee, and one is owned by Mrs. L. D. Yeaman at Carthage, whose late husband was a student of prehistoric villages and Indian remains.

Where the road from Tucker's Cross Roads to Bellwood crosses the old Rome Pike, is the famous Big Spring, which runs eighteen hundred gallons of water a minute to form the head of Cedar Creek. Here, in the natural amphitheater around the spring, the Cumberland Presbyterians held their great camp

This sandstone image was found on the site of a prehistoric Indian Village near Greenwood in Wilson County.

meetings in the early 1800s. Famous preachers, including the
Reverend Thomas Calhoun, were converted in these stormy,
colorful meetings. "The very leaves on the trees," Calhoun wrote
later, "seemed tinged with a Saviour's blood." Thousands of
people traveled, on horseback and on foot, to hear the long,
fiery sermons.

About four miles northwest of Lebanon, on the Coles Ferry
Pike, is the site of a famous Methodist campground called
Ebenezer. A generation before the Civil War, when the camp
meetings were at their peak of popularity, people crowded the
campground. All that is left of this campground today is a lonely
cemetery set on top of a wooded hill.

REELFOOT LAKE

There are two accounts of how Reelfoot Lake was formed, and a brochure by the Tennessee Conservation Department says the Indian legend "seems more popular to the public."

Chief Reelfoot, a warrior of the Chickasaw tribe, in the course of his hunting trips, met and fell violently in love with Starlight, a princess of the Choctaws. Starlight's stern father refused his permission for her marriage to Reelfoot, so Reelfoot and his braves stole her away. The Indian gods, however, did not approve. As the Chickasaws celebrated the success of Reelfoot's venture, the earth opened up and swallowed the whole tribe.

The earth did "open up," and that's about the only truth in the legend. Reelfoot Lake was formed by the great New Madrid earthquake of 1811-1812.

The first shock of this great disaster came on the night of December 16, 1811, with the center of the disturbance near New Madrid, Missouri, about fifteen miles west of the Mississippi river. John Bradbury, the English naturalist and a friend of Thomas Jefferson, was aboard a boat on the Mississippi when the earthquake struck. He described the crash of falling trees and the screaming of wild fowl on the river. At times during the quake the great stream changed its course and even the direction of its flow. Huge bluffs broke loose from the banks and fell into the water. Tennessee's historian, S. C. Williams, wrote of this great quake:

"As the region of occurrence was unsettled, West Tennessee almost wholly so, there was but a small loss of life; consequently comparatively little attention was given to it, though scientific

219

literature, in this country and in Europe, has given it a place among the great earthquakes of the world."

It was generally thought that the great tremor of December 16 was not the shock that created Reelfoot Lake—other earthquakes followed. On February 7, 1812, came the greatest shock of all, with its center on the eastern bank of the Mississippi.

In Nashville Andrew Jackson wrote, on February 8, that the quake was such as "to throw down chimneys and to crack walls." He commented that "few boats will venture the passage down the Mississippi this spring," and he feared that many boats on the river at the time were lost—as indeed many were.

Williams noted that "it is probable that it was this shock that created the great subsidence which formed Reelfoot Lake—a fact unknown to the residents of nearby New Madrid for years." A letter written by Eliza Bryan from New Madrid in 1816 said that "lately it has been discovered that a lake was formed on the opposite side of the Mississippi in the Indian country." Truly but little was known of this "Indian country," though it was in this region that David Crockett won much of his fame as a hunter. Reelfoot Lake was not mentioned in the *Tennessee Gazeteer* of 1834, though it had been there for twenty-two years. Reelfoot River is mentioned as a branch of the Obion River.

It was Reelfoot River, sometimes "Creek," which was blocked by the quake to form the lake. Killebrew's *Resources of Tennessee* notes that "at the same time that the old channel of Reelfoot Creek was dammed up, it is supposed that the area of country now covered by the lake sank several feet, and that the depression was gradually filled with the water which was prevented from flowing into the Mississippi.

"The bed of the lake is in some places not less than twenty or even thirty feet below the level of the surrounding country. The trunks of dead trees abundantly confirm this view, as their roots are to be found from ten to thirty feet below the surface of the water."

Almost a century ago Killebrew noted that "the lake is a favorite resort of wild fowls in the fall and winter . . . every year a few swans are seen." He added that "tons of fish and thousands of ducks and geese" were shipped to various markets from Reelfoot. Killebrew saw no reason why the place should not be as popular as Long Branch and Saratoga. "At present," he went on, "accommodations for visitors are very poor, and are not of themselves at all attractive."

Little Lake County, next to Trousdale and the smallest in the state, lies hemmed in between Reelfoot Lake and the Mississippi. This county, formed in 1870, was formerly a part of Obion, which had contained the entire lake before that date. In the early years of the state, residents of the land between the lake and river were almost cut off from the world and were excused from military drill except in time of war.

Reelfoot Lake is about three miles wide and eighteen miles long, and it is still a favorite with fishermen and duck hunters. The "night rider" shooting of 1908, the result of a feud over fishing rights, was one of the dark chapters in the history of Reelfoot. A book by Paul Vanderwood, *Night Riders of Reelfoot Lake,* published in 1969, has a complete account of the night rider violence.

Today Reelfoot is peaceful, though shotguns pop and ducks come tumbling down in the fall. A Tennessee state park is located along the shore of the lake on State Highways 21 and 22, a mile east of Tiptonville.

Picnic sites are favorite spots along the shore under the big Cypress trees. The Cypress "knees" and water plants are to be found everywhere in this wild and beautiful country, and at times swarms of blackbirds darken the sky. A state museum building houses a collection of Indian artifacts and specimens of wildlife found in the area. Other attractions include a kiddie land, excursion boats, and tent camping.

Despite the modern "improvements" Reelfoot is still a natural wonder, a great work of nature. Its finest features are the wide green waters, the great Cypresses, the bream and largemouth bass, and the ducks that come honking in when there's winter in the air and ice on the water.

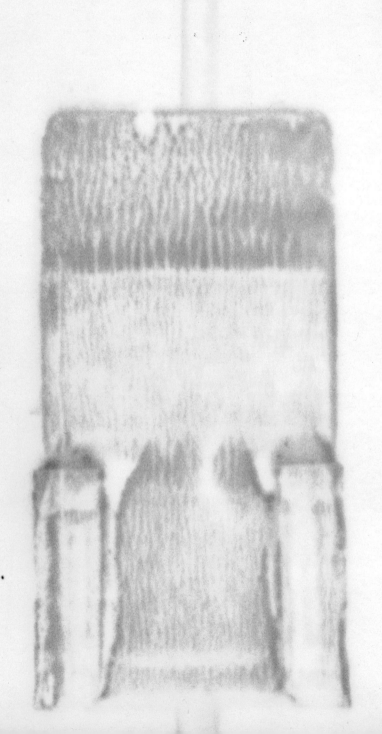

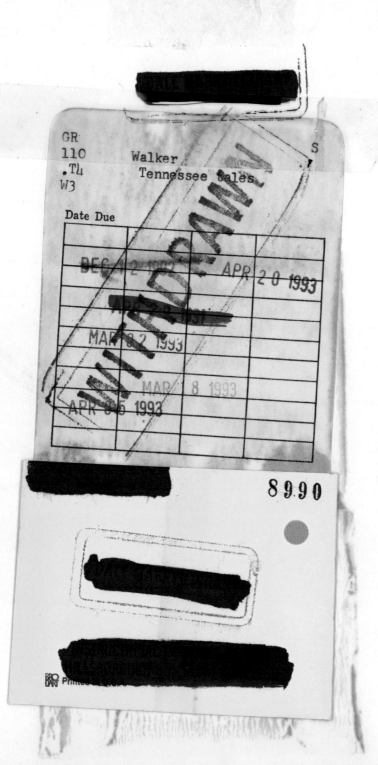